D0777353

Usborne

ILLUSTRATED
BIBLE
STORIES

Usborne

ILLUSTRATED
BIBLE
STORIES

Illustrated by John Joven

Contents

The New Testament   253

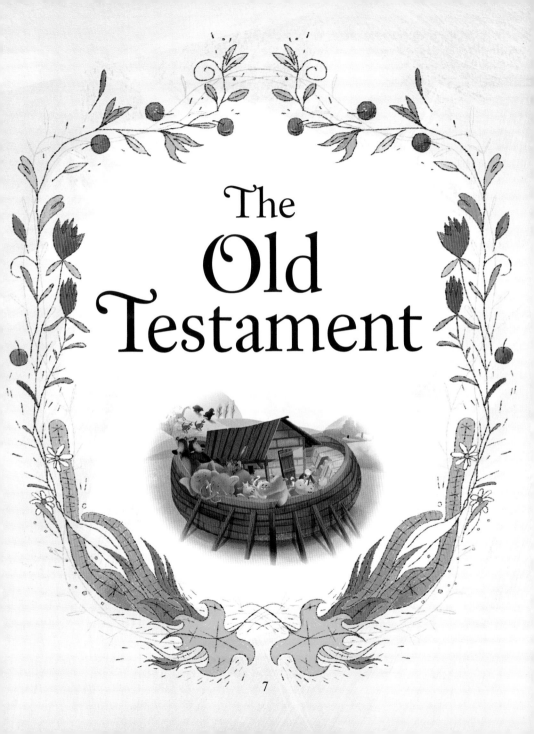

The
Old
Testament

About the Old Testament

The Old Testament is a massive collection of stories, poems and rules for living life. At its heart is God, the creator of the world.

God loves His world, and constantly calls on the people He put in it to listen to Him and talk to Him. But only a few answer.

The heroes of the Old Testament are the women and men who do listen, and who fight against every obstacle to do what God asks.

One of God's earliest champions is an old man named Abram, whom God later renames

Abraham. Many of the best-loved tales in the Old Testament are about Abraham and his family, down many generations.

Abraham's grandson, Jacob, is given the name 'Israel' by God – and so the children of Jacob's twelve sons become known as Israelites.

They battle enemy kings and armies who worship rival gods. They fight with friends and family who struggle to listen to God. And, sometimes, they wrestle with their own doubts, and argue with God Himself.

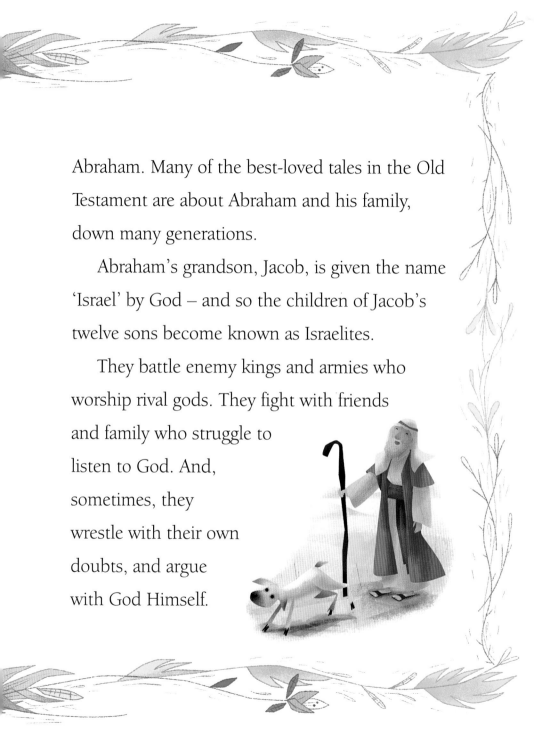

Adam and Eve

Adam and Eve

In the beginning, everything was dark, cold and empty, until God created Heaven and the Earth.

God hovered over the dark waters that covered the Earth and said, "Let there be light."

And there was light.

God was pleased with what He had done but He wasn't finished yet. Next, He separated the light from the darkness, and called the light, day, and the darkness, night. As the darkness rolled over the Earth, the first day turned into the first night.

Adam and Eve

On the second day, He created the sky to arch over the waters of the Earth. The hours passed as He worked, and soon, night came for the second time.

The following morning, He parted the waters so that dry land could appear and named the waters, seas. He was happy with the land and the seas of His brand new world. But He did not stop to rest.

"Plants, grow up from the ground," said God. "Produce fruits, and seeds so that new plants can grow."

All over the Earth, lush, green plants grew and bore ripe fruits, and God saw that it was good.

That was the third day.

On the fourth day, God made two great lights, one for the day and one for the night, and He placed them in the sky. The day's light was hotter and brighter and He called it the Sun. The paler light that shone at night He called the Moon. God looked upon the flaming Sun and the mysterious Moon and He felt glad.

During the fifth day, He created birds to fly in the sky, and fish to swim in the seas. Great whales leaped up in joy, to splash back down into the depths. Tiny fish teemed everywhere, and the air was full of the sound of flapping wings. Then, as the Sun set, the new birds nestled down to sleep, the blue seas became dark and the fifth day ended.

Dawn broke on the sixth day. God began creating animals to roam through all the lands of the Earth, from slow, gentle cows and roaring tigers to tiny creeping insects and scurrying mice.

"Go out into the world and multiply," God told them. "Have babies and fill the Earth with animals."

And still He wasn't finished.

"Now I will make a creature that is more like Me than any other," He said. "I will make a human being." So saying, God took a handful of dust from the ground and breathed life into it. The creature took shape and became Adam, the very first man.

God smiled at His new creation. "Adam," He said, "it is your job to look after all the animals and birds and plants and everything else on Earth. You must give them all names, and they will obey you."

"Thank You, God," said Adam, but he looked a little sad. God realized that he was lonely.

"I will make a companion for you," God said. At that moment, Adam fell into a deep, deep sleep. God took one of the ribs from Adam's chest and shaped it into a human form.

"This is Eve," said God, when Adam woke up. "She is a woman, and you will both live together in a garden I have made, named Eden. You will have children together and fill the Earth with people."

Adam and Eve entered the garden of Eden and looked around in wonder. Eden was dazzlingly lovely, full of ripe fruit and bright flowers. The air was heavy with the scent of nectar and honey.

God pointed to a tree in the middle of the garden.

"You may eat the fruit of any bush or tree in this garden, except the one in the middle," He said, "for that is the Tree of Knowledge. Anyone who eats its fruit will gain knowledge of good and evil, and that is forbidden. If you disobey Me, you will die."

Adam and Eve promised they would never eat the forbidden fruit. God looked at the two humans, and at everything that He had made, and He saw that it was all very good indeed. As the Sun set, He knew His work was finished.

On the seventh day, God – and everything on His

Earth – rested. Adam and Eve gazed in delight at all the beautiful animals and plants that God had made for them. They were naked, but they saw nothing wrong with that. They didn't even have a word for "naked" yet. It was just the way things were.

Time passed in the garden of Eden. Adam and Eve cared for the animals and plucked plump, ripe fruit from the trees whenever they were hungry.

One day, a serpent came creeping on soft feet through the garden. Eve watched as it approached, wondering what it might want.

The serpent reared up on its hind legs and spoke in a hissing whisper, as gentle as a kiss. "Is it true that God told you that you can't eat the fruit of every tree in this wonderful garden?"

"He said we may eat from every tree," said Eve,

Adam and Eve

"except for the tree in the very middle of Eden. God says if we eat fruit from that tree, we will die."

"You won't die," said the serpent. "God is lying to you. In truth, God won't let you eat from the tree because He knows that the moment you do, your eyes will be opened to all the wonders of the universe. You will be like gods, knowing good and evil." The serpent shook his head. "It doesn't seem right that only God should be the one to know everything. He treats you like children."

Eve paused. She looked at the tree and considered the serpent's words. It certainly didn't look as though the fruit would kill her – in fact, it looked delicious. "Surely wisdom isn't such a bad thing?" said Eve. So she walked to the Tree of Knowledge, plucked a fruit and sank her teeth into it. It *was* delicious.

"Adam, come here, I have something for you," she called, holding out the fruit. Adam took a bite.

"Which tree is it from?" he asked, although he already knew.

Moments later, they both knew everything. They suddenly realized that they were naked, and felt a pang of shame.

"We must cover ourselves," said Adam, grabbing a handful of leaves from the nearest tree. "These fig leaves should do."

They sewed the large fig leaves together to cover themselves, but they were still ashamed.

"Adam, where are you?" came a voice. It was the voice that Adam and Eve had been dreading ever since they bit into the fruit of the forbidden tree.

"We have to hide," whispered Eve, and they ran

away into the trees.

"Come out," said God. "I can see you hiding."

So they came out of their hiding place. Adam spoke to God, "I heard Your voice and I was ashamed because I was naked, so I hid."

"Who said you were naked?" asked God.

Adam and Eve did not reply.

"Have you eaten the fruit of the forbidden tree?" God asked. "After I ordered you not to?"

Adam scowled and pointed to Eve. "The woman You gave to me did this. She offered me the fruit, so I ate it."

God said to Eve, "Is this true? Did you do this?"

Eve could not look up. She looked to the ground, where she'd first seen the serpent. "I couldn't help it. The snake tricked me into eating it," she said.

"Serpent!" roared God, in a voice of thunder and fury.

The serpent came slinking out from the long grass. It did not look up, it merely hissed to itself.

"Because you did this, worm, you are cursed," said God. "You will always crawl on your belly and eat dust all the days of your life."

The serpent tried to rear up on its hind legs in defiance, but it could not. Its legs had disappeared.

"And," said God, "I will make it so that you and the woman are enemies forever, and her children and her children's children will hate you and try to crush you. You, in turn, will bite them."

The serpent slithered away, hissing curses of its own about the unfairness of its fate. "I will have my revenge," it swore.

To Eve, God said, "I will make childbirth a painful thing for you. You will cling to your husband, and he will rule over you."

To Adam, He said, "Because you ate the forbidden fruit, I will curse the soil, so that growing your food will be a terrible burden. The ground will be full of thistles and thorns and you will have to sweat and suffer to grow your food. This is what your life will be like until you die and are buried in the ground."

God looked at Adam and Eve, angry and sad at once. "I told you that you would die if you ate the fruit. Now, one day, you shall. I made you out of dust, and to dust you will return."

God took some pity on them and gave them clothes made from warm animal skins, but He could not let them stay in Eden. He spoke, in a voice that all

creation could hear, saying,
"Look. Humans have become
like gods. So now, in case
they also reach out for
the fruit on the Tree of
Life, I must send them
away. Anyone who eats
from the Tree of Life will
live forever, and I cannot
allow that, now that they
have eaten the forbidden fruit."

So God drove out Adam and Eve from the garden
of Eden. He summoned fierce angels to watch over
the gate. The new angelic guards took up their post,
wielding mighty swords of fire to protect the garden
of Eden and keep everyone away.

Adam and Eve

Sunk in misery, Adam and Eve walked out into the wild world beyond the garden, to begin their new life. They could never go home again.

Noah's
Ark

Noah's Ark

Many years had passed since God had created the world. The number of people living in it grew and grew. But they were greedy, selfish, vicious and violent, forever plotting evil schemes. God knew they were wicked, and felt sorry He had ever made them.

At last, God came to a decision. "I created people," He said, "but I can also destroy them. I will wash them from the face of the Earth."

Out of all the people on Earth, there was just one old man who was not evil. His name was Noah. God noticed Noah, and saw that he had an honest heart. He worked hard, cared for his family and respected others – but most of all, he loved God.

So God formed a plan.

"Noah," said God, "the time has come for me to wash evil things from the Earth and destroy them completely. I will send a vast flood, the greatest there has ever been. All living things on Earth will die, but you and your family will be saved.

You must build a huge ark from wood. I will show you how. Then, fill it with food and drink, and take on board every kind of animal there is, a male and a female of each. Inside the ark, I will keep you all safe."

Noah was a good man, so he did as God said. He drew up plans, gathered wood and started to build.

He sawed and planed and hammered and fitted. It was a long, hard job – after all, the ark had to be big enough to hold two of every kind of animal on the Earth. Noah's three sons, Shem, Ham and Japheth, helped out and, at long last, the ark was finished. It was huge, with dozens of rooms, and sealed inside and out with waterproof pitch. There were windows to see out of, a big door in the side, stacks of every kind of food, and barrels of drinking water, all exactly as God had requested.

Noah looked at the vast ark, nodded with satisfaction, and waited to see what would happen next.

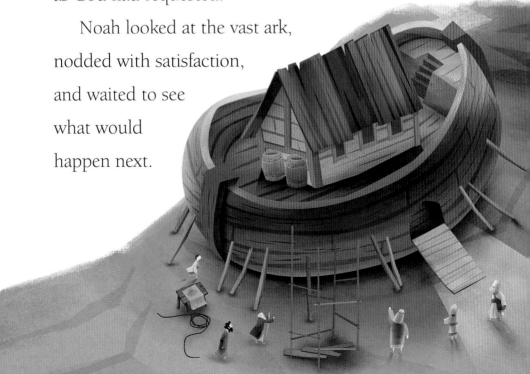

He had no idea how to gather the animals into the ark, and he certainly had no idea how to make the ark float when the flood came. But he knew God would find a way. He didn't have to wait long.

With roars and trumpets, squeaks, squawks, howls and hisses, a huge crowd of animals, all in pairs, ran, trotted, waddled, slithered, soared, crept and buzzed into view. Noah knew just what to do.

"No pushing please!" he called. "That's it, form a line, two by two, watch the little ones, straight ahead and up the ramp, plenty of room for everyone!"

Just as Noah asked, all the animals went in an orderly line into the ark. Noah and his family – his wife, his three sons and their wives – followed the animals inside. With an echoing bang, the great door slammed shut behind them.

Inside the ark, it was cool and dim. The birds fluttered and clucked softly as they found perches on the rafters. The bees buzzed into a knothole in a plank, the snails crawled halfway up a beam, the snakes sunned themselves in front of a window and the penguins found a shady corner.

The horses, lions and giraffes rustled gently as they nestled into their straw bedding. Every now and then, the timbers creaked as the elephants and rhinos shifted their weight on their great feet. Noah and his family sat down wherever there was space. They listened to the noises of the animals and they waited...

They waited for seven whole days. Then, they heard a new sound. At first, it was a faint pattering, but as it grew to a loud and steady drumming, they realized it was the sound of raindrops.

Before long, the rain was coming down not just in drops, but in sheets, torrents and cascades. Never had there been a downpour like it. For forty days and forty nights, it rained. And, as it rained, the waters of the Earth swelled and rose, creeping closer and closer to the ark. It swayed and tilted, and then, with a great heave, it was lifted up on the rising flood, riding along on the waves.

And the water kept rising. First, the valleys, then the hills and, finally, the very tallest mountains were submerged beneath the churning ocean. Still the storm raged on and on, until the entire face of the Earth was covered by the flood. Everything and everyone outside the ark was washed away.

Noah's Ark

Noah's Ark

At last, God sent a breeze over the surface of the waters and they were calmed. It stopped raining, the seas stopped rising and the sun came out.

Noah stood at a window and looked out. As far as he could see, in every direction, the sunshine glinted off a vast, unending sea.

But, over the days that followed, it seemed to Noah that the waters were slowly drying up and draining away.

"I know what I'll do," he thought, "I'll send out a bird, and watch where it goes. From high in the sky, it should be able to spot the nearest dry land – if there *is* any land yet."

Noah chose a raven from the ark and released it into the bright, clear air. It flew around the ark in bigger and bigger circles, searching in every direction.

Gradually, it dwindled to a tiny speck, and then became too far away to see at all.

The raven never returned.

Noah was disappointed, but he knew he had to try again. This time, he released a dove. Just like the raven, the dove circled and circled around the ark, getting smaller and smaller. Noah felt his heart sink as it disappeared over the horizon. But, hours later, he heard a shout of excitement. The dove was flying back to the ark, carrying something green in its beak. As the dove flew closer, Noah could see that it was holding a tiny branch from an olive tree.

"There must be dry land somewhere," he shouted. "Trees are growing again!"

He gave the dove food and water, and let her rest for seven days. "You've done well," he told her, "but I need to ask you one more thing. Fly out again for me and show me where the nearest land can be found."

The little dove soared off again, but this time she flew in a straight line. Noah followed her with his aged eyes. There, on the horizon, he could see tips of land sticking up above the water. They were the topmost peaks of a great mountain range.

Noah's knees went weak with happiness. "Land, dry land ahead!" he shouted. Everyone crowded around eagerly to look.

Moments later, the ark gave a huge, crunching shudder. The animals squealed in alarm and dashed back inside for cover, but Noah wasn't afraid.

"Our prayers are answered," he said. "The ark has

come to rest. Soon, the long wait will be over."

Sure enough, just as he said, the day soon came when dry land could be seen on every side. God spoke to Noah once more.

"Leave the ark now, Noah," He said. "Go with your wife and your sons and their wives. Take all the animals, too. All of you, go out into the new, clean Earth. Spread out far and wide, settle down and have families, so the lands will be fruitful once again."

So Noah and his family and the animals

did exactly as God said.

But God had not quite finished with Noah. He blessed him and his sons, and spoke to them again, one last time.

"I will make a promise to all of you, for all time," He said. "I will never again cover the whole Earth with a flood. As a sign of this promise, I give you this

rainbow. Every time you see it, you must remember the promise I have made, and I will do the same."

The Tower of Babel

The Tower of Babel

Long after Noah and his family had left the ark, a bustling young city was gripped by the excitement of a new invention.

"Behold!" said a builder to the crowd, who were clustering around to admire the house he had just built. "It's made of *bricks*. I made them by baking mud in the sun. They're much stronger and easier to build with than wood."

"That's incredible!" gasped people in the crowd. "Just think of what we can build now!"

The Tower of Babel

It wasn't long before grand, mud-brick buildings were springing up everywhere. People took great pride in making each of their buildings larger and stronger than the ones before.

One day, the mayor called a meeting. "Our buildings are bigger and better than ever," he said, a little smugly. "But the question is: what can we build to make our city truly great?"

"I have an idea," said an architect. "Let's build an enormous tower right in the middle."

"Yes!" cheered the others. "It will be so tall that our city will be famous all around the world! Everyone will see how clever we are."

"Very well. Work shall begin tomorrow morning," proclaimed the mayor.

Meanwhile, God was watching the meeting.

"There's nothing wrong with being ambitious and inventive," He thought, "I just hope they don't get carried away."

At first, all went well. Each day, the people worked hard on the tower, laying brick upon brick from dawn until dusk.

After a few weeks, the mayor stopped by to speak to the architect. "Are we making good progress?" he asked. "It certainly looks like it," he added, gazing up at the tower, which was already soaring above everything else in the city.

"It's now the tallest tower ever built," replied the architect, feeling very pleased with himself.

"Good, but our people want it to be even higher," said the mayor. "It should be so tall that, from the top, people on the ground look like tiny little ants."

God was still watching, and He was beginning to tire of their arrogance. "It's one thing to be proud of your achievements, but they are starting to think they can do anything," He thought.

The tower grew taller and taller.

"Goodness!" exclaimed the mayor, the next time he came past. "I can't even see the top."

"And we haven't finished yet," boasted the architect.

"Of course you haven't," said the mayor. "The people want it to be so tall that they can look down on the clouds. And don't forget: our people always get what they want."

God, watching on from Heaven, was losing patience. "They need to realize that humans have limits..." He thought. "I wonder if they will ever see sense."

But still the people weren't satisfied. Even after the tower broke through the clouds, they wanted more.

"If we just go a little higher," they said excitedly, "we'll be able to climb up to the top and step into Heaven itself."

At this, God had heard enough. "They've become so arrogant, they think they're as powerful as Me. It's time to put them back in their place," He decided.

The next morning, the people started work on the tower again.

"Can you help me with this ladder?" one builder said to the others.

But instead of helping, they simply stared blankly at him.

"That's odd..." thought the builder, struggling

with the ladder on his own.

He put it up against the tower and started climbing. He had only gone a few steps when he realized he hadn't brought a chisel, so he called down to the others, "Hey, can one of you pass me a chisel?"

The people down below looked confused. One of them shrugged and offered up a trowel.

"No, no, I asked for a chisel!" shouted the man. "What's the matter with you all today?"

The people below opened their mouths to reply, but what came out took everyone by surprise.

"Cosa vuoi dire?" said one.

"Chan eil mi gad thuigsinn!" said another.

"Co tým myslíš?" said a third.

"Huh?" said the builder. "What's going on? Why

The Tower of Babel

are you all speaking so strangely?"

But nobody could understand what he, or anyone else, was saying. Each person spoke, but it sounded like gibberish to everyone else.

"Hey! What are you saying?" said the builder, growing more and more frustrated. "Are you making fun of me?"

The others went on talking in their own languages, and they too started getting very annoyed when they realized nothing they said was understood.

The exasperated builder lost his temper. "Hey!" he said again. "Stop it! Stop it or I'll..."

He climbed down the ladder and struck one of the others on the nose. "That'll quieten him," he thought. But just as he was congratulating himself, someone else clonked him on the head. By the time he came to his senses, everyone around him was squabbling and brawling.

"Oh no," wailed the architect. "Stop! Calm down. Get back to work. Please!" But it was no good – he was speaking his own language just like everyone else.

"We can't live like this. We're ruined! This city, the tower... Everything is ruined," cried the mayor.

And indeed it was. The people abandoned the tower and left the city, speaking their own languages as they went. They moved to different places all over the world, and built new towns and cities wherever they settled. As for the deserted tower, it was soon overgrown with weeds, and became known as the Tower of Babel after the 'babbling' people who began it.

Abram and Lot

Abram and Lot

Abram was a rich, old man. He hadn't been born with money – he believed it was his reward for always obeying God's will. He was married to a beautiful woman, Sarai. He owned thousands of animals and commanded hundreds of servants to look after them. The only thing he didn't have was a child.

Some years before, God had promised Abram that he wouldn't have just one child, he would have many children. Abram didn't doubt the God he loved, but he and Sarai were already old, and he was beginning to grow impatient.

He was so grumpy, he even began arguing with his beloved nephew, Lot. When Lot's father died, Abram had taken the boy in. But Lot was now a grown man, with his own young family, and it was time for uncle and nephew to part ways.

"Lot, you are like a son to me," Abram said, "and I want to give you an inheritance. Take half of all my animals and servants, go out, and make your way in the world. Whichever path you choose, I'll go in the other direction."

Lot went east, to a land beyond the hills known as Jordan. He settled with his wife, two daughters and all their animals close to a pair of cities called Sodom and Gomorrah.

So Abram headed west, deep into a land named Canaan. When he reached the middle, God spoke to him. "Abram, I promise you, all this land shall belong to your children, your children's children, and their children, too. You shall be a father and grandfather to so many children that no one will ever be able to count them all!"

Abram built an altar on top of a hill to glorify God, and pitched a tent beside it, where he and his wife Sarai lived happily.

Lot, meanwhile, was not so happy. Sodom and Gomorrah turned out to be home to some of the most wicked people on Earth. Even worse, Lot found himself caught up in a war. A powerful king from a land beyond the eastern mountains had raised an army and was poised to attack the two cities.

A fierce battle broke out, and the invading army managed to chase Sodom's soldiers into a vast pit of

slime, where they all drowned. Bera, the king of
Sodom, surrendered. The invading king stole his gold,
and kidnapped many people to sell as slaves –
including Lot and his family.

Word reached Abram in Canaan that his beloved
nephew was in trouble. He gathered together his
servants, over three hundred in all, and rode to the
rescue. In the middle of the night, Abram and his
servants killed the army while they slept. Triumphant,
they returned to Sodom with all the gold and
everyone who had been kidnapped.

King Bera was so grateful, he got down on his
knees and praised Abram's God. Then he turned to
Abram. "Mighty Abram, slayer of my enemies, please
take with you all the gold that you brought back."

"I will not," said Abram, firmly. "I do not wish to

take any gift from you, not so much as a shoelace! You men of Sodom are a disgrace to God, and I want nothing to do with you."

Eager to leave the wicked place, Abram returned to Canaan at once, but Lot decided to stay in Sodom.

That night, God appeared to Abram while he was asleep. "Abram, wake up. You have served me well, and I have a great reward for you."

For the first time in his life, Abram answered back. "You have already made a great promise to me – that my children shall rule Canaan. But I don't *have* any children!"

"Look up, Abram," said God. "Look up at the heavens, and tell me how many stars you can see."

"There are too many to count," Abram replied.

"That is how many children you shall be a father

to," said God. "To make a sign of my promise, I give you a new name – Abraham. And, from now on, your wife will be called Sarah."

But, twelve months later, Abram and Sarai – now Abraham and Sarah – were still childless.

One day, Abraham was resting from the midday sun in the shade beside his tent, when three strangers appeared in the distance. Quick to be helpful and kind, he rose to greet them. "Please, won't you stop for a while? Have some water to drink, and rest with me here."

"We will," said the strangers.

Abraham and Sarah busied themselves fetching water, baking bread and preparing a meal to feed their guests. After everyone had eaten their fill, Sarah went into her tent while the men sat outside, talking.

"Abraham," began the first stranger, "I have a prediction for you. We three will come to visit you again in nine months' time – and by then, your wife will have given birth to a son."

From inside the tent, Abraham and the three men heard a peal of laughter. Sarah's voice came through loud and clear. "What nonsense are you talking! I'm an old woman – do you seriously expect me to have a child?"

"Is anything too difficult for God?" replied the stranger. Sarah was speechless, and felt guilty for daring to laugh at God.

"We must leave you now," said the second stranger, solemnly. "We have important business in Sodom."

"Let me show you the way," said Abraham, pointing out a path that wound down the hill. Abraham watched as the men walked away, only to see an amazing sight – God himself appeared on the hillside and beckoned to the strangers. At that moment, Abraham realized that these were no ordinary men, but angels.

"I've decided to let Abraham hear My plan," God told his angels. "He is kind and loyal – the most righteous man who ever lived, and he deserves to hear the truth.

I will stay here to talk to him, while you go down to Sodom and Gomorrah. See if those cities really are as wretched, wicked and sinful as we have heard. And if it *is* true – burn them to the ground!"

As the angels made their way down the hillside, Abraham stumbled forward and spoke to God. "Is that truly Your plan, Lord God? Will You really destroy those two vast cities? What about the decent people who live there? Is it fair to punish them along with the wicked? Suppose You find just fifty righteous people among the thousands who live in Sodom and Gomorrah. Do they have to die, too?"

God answered, "If I find fifty righteous people in Sodom, I will spare the whole city."

Abraham shuffled his feet and looked down at the ground, not daring to catch God's eye. "I am nothing compared to You," he said, trembling with fear, "but I can't keep silent. What if Sodom is just five people

short of the fifty? Would You judge it fair to destroy it if there were forty-five good people who live there?"

"I will not destroy Sodom if I find forty-five good people," said God.

"But," continued Abraham, "what if there are just forty?"

"I will not destroy Sodom if I find forty good people there."

"But maybe You will only find thirty good people in Sodom. What then?"

"I will not destroy it for the sake of those thirty."

Abraham was now shaking with fear. Still not brave enough to look up, he spoke again. "B-but suppose there are only twenty righteous people in Sodom?"

"I will not destroy it for the sake of those twenty righteous people," replied God, patiently.

Abraham spoke up one last time, mustering all his courage to look up at God's face. "Please, God, don't be angry with me, but I have to ask You – what if You find just *ten* righteous men in all of Sodom?"

Once again, God answered calmly. "If I find just ten righteous people in all of Sodom, I will spare the whole city." With that, He left Abraham to collapse on the ground, astonished at the thought of his own boldness before God.

Down in the valley, the angels had arrived at the gates of Sodom. By now, it was late into the evening, and the streets were dark. Lot, who lived close by the city gates, saw the angels and ran out of his house.

"Strangers, I bid you welcome to Sodom. Please, come into my home. You're most welcome to stay with me tonight."

"Thank you for your kind offer," they replied, "but we'd really prefer to stay out in the street, and observe the city."

"But you can't!" Lot exclaimed. "It's too dangerous. The people of Sodom aren't friendly to outsiders. Please, come and stay with me."

No sooner had the angels agreed, than a crowd gathered outside Lot's house, banging loudly on the front door.

"Hey, Lot, open up!" shouted the crowd. "Where are those strangers you let in a minute ago? We want to meet them."

Lot feared for his guests' lives. He knew the crowd meant harm. So he opened the door and begged, "Please, leave them alone. If you really need some entertainment for this evening, I'll send my daughters down so they can sing and dance for you. These visitors are under my protection."

"We don't want your daughters. We want those outsiders!" screamed the mob, reaching out and seizing Lot by his cloak.

From behind, the angels grabbed Lot and wrestled him back inside the house. One of them stood in the door frame and held out his arm menacingly. At once, a flash of light flew out and blinded all those at the front of the crowd. They howled in pain and ran away. People at the back muttered vile curses, but they were too afraid to attack Lot's house again.

"Lot, you must leave this city tonight," said the angels. "Take your wife and your daughters and get out of here. Don't take anything with you, and, most important of all, don't look back!"

Lot waited just long enough for the crowd to return to their homes, then he and his family slipped out of the city and up into the hills. As the dawn began to break, Lot heard tremendous, terrible noises coming from the city behind him.

God's angels had summoned a rain of fire and a hail of foul-smelling, burning rocks that fell from the sky in a great storm of destruction. Explosions shook the valley as every building in Sodom and Gomorrah was completely and utterly burned to the ground.

High up on the mountain, Lot and his family were

Abram and Lot

safe from the flames. As the angels had commanded, Lot hid his eyes from the awesome sight of God's wrath. But his wife could not resist looking back down on Sodom. In that very instant, she turned into a pillar of salt. Her body disintegrated in the wind, and her remains blew across the desolate valley.

Lot was haunted by the death of his wife and lived out the rest of his days in a quiet mountain town, looked after by his devoted daughters.

On the far side of the valley, in Canaan, Abraham and Sarah had watched the sky turn from pink to red to gold and finally to black, as a great cloud of soot and ash rose to the sky, scattering the remains of the wicked cities of Sodom and Gomorrah. They huddled outside their tent, fearful of God's vengeance. They prayed that by the time their son was born, the world would be a happier place.

Abraham and Isaac

Abraham and Isaac

All Abraham and Sarah wanted was to have a baby. But even after angels told them that Sarah would have a son in nine months' time, they could hardly believe it. They trusted God to keep His word, but Sarah was ninety and Abraham was nearly a hundred years old. It seemed impossible.

A few days after the angels' visit, Abraham heard Sarah crying.

"What's the matter?" he asked, rushing over.

Sarah looked up at her husband through tear-filled eyes. "It's happened," she whispered.

Abraham and Isaac

"We're going to have a baby."

At long last, God had given Abraham and Sarah what they wanted most of all.

When the baby was born, Abraham and Sarah named him Isaac, as God asked. Abraham didn't miss a moment of Isaac's childhood, and watched him grow into a healthy, strong boy. Every night, Isaac came and sat by Abraham and they talked for hours. Abraham often remembered what God had told him: one day, Isaac would marry, and Abraham would have as many grandchildren and great-grandchildren as there were stars in the sky.

"Isaac, I'm going to the market," Sarah said one day. "Would you help me carry the shopping?"

"Of course," Isaac replied cheerfully.

Abraham waved goodbye and sat down, looking

out over the hills of Canaan, deep in thought. He'd had a long life and it hadn't been an unhappy one, but it was only recently that he felt as if the last piece had slotted into place. Since Isaac had been born, he felt calm and unafraid. God had promised great things for Isaac, so Abraham had nothing to worry about.

But then, a mighty voice shook him from his dreaming. "Abraham, where are you?" God was calling him.

"I am here, Lord," said Abraham quickly.

"Abraham, what I am about to ask you to do will not be easy," said God.

"I'll do anything!" Abraham said. Whatever it was that God wanted him to do, he couldn't imagine refusing.

"Tomorrow morning, you must travel to a place

called Moriah," God continued. "There, you must make a sacrifice."

Abraham had made sacrifices many times before. It was a ritual that was always done in the same way: an animal was killed with a knife and then burned as an offering to God.

Abraham was happy to do it. "Of course!" he cried. "I have two fat young lambs, or a goat, or..."

But he was cut off. "I don't want you to sacrifice a lamb or a goat, Abraham. You must sacrifice your son, Isaac."

Abraham felt sick. He didn't understand how God could ask him to take any young boy's life, never mind his own son's. God gave Isaac to Abraham and Sarah: was He now going to take him away?

Abraham couldn't bear the thought of giving up

his son. But he also couldn't stand the thought of going against something that God wanted. He knew he should trust and obey God, but surely this was too awful a thing to demand.

When Isaac arrived home with his mother, chattering and laughing, he noticed at once that something was wrong. His father was pale and shaking. "Isaac, go to your bed now, and go to sleep," Abraham said. "We have a long journey ahead of us in the morning."

"But it's early!" Isaac protested.

"Now!" Abraham shouted. Isaac ran to his bed, upset and confused. His father had never shouted at him before.

"What's wrong?" asked Sarah, once Isaac had left. "Did something happen while we were at the market?"

But Abraham knew that this was a burden he must carry alone. He couldn't tell Sarah what God had asked him to do.

"Prepare my donkey," he said gruffly. "And ask two of our men to be ready in the morning. We're going to Moriah to offer a sacrifice."

Sarah didn't dare ask any more questions. She did as her husband wanted. That night, she lay silently next to him in the dark and wondered what could possibly be making the sacrifice so urgent.

The next morning, Sarah woke early and realized that Abraham wasn't beside her. From outside, she heard a *thud, thud, thud.* Looking through the tent's opening, she saw Abraham stooped over the wood block, angrily chopping firewood.

Puzzled, she rose and went to Isaac. "It's time to wake up," she said, gently shaking him. "You're going on a trip."

Isaac dressed hurriedly and went out to meet his father. Abraham was waiting for him, with the two servants and a donkey with two huge bundles of sticks balanced on its back.

"Father, where's the lamb for us to sacrifice?" asked Isaac. Abraham said nothing. Isaac knew better

than to ask again.

Normally, Isaac would have been excited about going on a trip with his father, but Abraham stayed silent and thoughtful as they set off. Isaac watched him as they walked. Abraham looked as if *he* were carrying all of the wood, instead of the donkey.

They walked for two days. At night, Abraham didn't talk and tell stories as he usually did. He stayed up praying while his son slept. He desperately wanted to understand why God had asked him to do such a terrible thing, but he wasn't getting any answers. All he could do was to keep going and trust in God. At the back of his mind he thought of what God had said about Isaac's future. It was some hope, at least, that Isaac might stay alive.

On the third day, Abraham saw Moriah on the

horizon. "Wait here with the donkey," he told the two servants. "Isaac and I will go on alone to the top of that hill to worship." He took the big bundles of firewood, placed them on Isaac's back, and together they kept walking.

"Father?" Isaac asked again. "Where's the lamb for us to sacrifice?"

"God will give us a lamb, Isaac," said Abraham.

Once they reached the top, Abraham stacked the wood with trembling hands until he had made a tall pyre. With every stick he placed, he hoped that something – anything – would happen to help him understand God's command.

But nothing happened. Abraham thought of life without Isaac. He could hardly bear it. But then he thought about living life knowing that his faith was

Abraham and Isaac

weak and small, and he couldn't bear that either.

"Come here, son," he said quietly to Isaac. Isaac ran over to him and Abraham lifted him into his arms and held him close. He could feel Isaac breathing quickly on his neck. Gently, Abraham laid his son down on top of the stack of wood.

"Father, what's happening?" Isaac said. "You're scaring me."

Abraham couldn't reply. Turning his eyes away, he drew a knife from his cloak and raised it high in the air...

"Abraham, where are you?" a voice rang out across the hillside.

Abraham froze. "I am here," he whispered.

"Put down your hand," said the angelic voice. "Isaac is safe. You were willing to give your son to

God. You've shown that you truly love Him."

Abraham dropped the knife, and it clattered to the ground. He grabbed Isaac and held him tightly, shaking and thanking God for keeping his son safe. They hugged each other on the top of the hill and let go only when they heard a rustling in the bushes behind them.

Abraham lifted his eyes. A ram was caught by its horns in a tree. Abraham went to free it, deciding he would sacrifice the ram instead of Isaac, to worship God.

Once he had made his sacrifice, the angel spoke to him again.

"You have done a truly good and righteous thing, Abraham," he said. "God will bless you and your family, and Isaac will grow up to have grandchildren and great-grandchildren who will spread God's word to every nation on the Earth. Each one of them will have God's blessing, too."

Abraham turned to his son. "Isaac, do you understand why I was willing to put your life in danger even though I love you beyond measure?" he asked.

"Yes, Father," replied Isaac. "It was because you trusted God and trusted that He would provide a way out."

"And so He did," said Abraham, smiling. "From now on, this place shall be known as Jehovah-Jireh, the Lord will provide."

Joseph and the Dreams

Joseph and the Dreams

"I had the strangest dream last night," said Joseph. He was at home with his brothers in their cramped house in the land of Canaan.

His brothers glared at him. "No one cares about your dreams," said one.

"Stop showing off," said another.

Joseph wasn't surprised at their reaction. Each one of his ten older half-brothers hated him and he was used to it.

He would often overhear his brothers whispering about him and calling him cruel names. The bullying had grown worse recently, after their father, Jacob, bought Joseph a beautiful and expensive coat. The coat was dyed in a rainbow of hues, and it shimmered in the sunlight.

Joseph stuck out his chin. "Let them be jealous," he thought. "It's not my fault Father loves me." So he decided to tell them his dream whether they wanted to hear it or not.

"I dreamed that we were in the fields, gathering grain," he began. Jacob and his sons were all farmers, so that was something they often did together.

A chorus of boos and catcalls followed, but Joseph went on. "We were tying up our crops into sheaves when my sheaf suddenly rose up and all of your sheaves bowed down to mine."

His brothers almost spat with fury. "Are you saying you plan to rule over us one day?"

"I'm just telling you my dream," said Joseph. But in his heart, he knew that there was something more to what he'd seen.

The next night, he dreamed again, and in the morning, he told his brothers, and his father too. "I dreamed that the Sun and Moon and stars were bowing down to me," said Joseph.

Jacob shooed him away. "Are you trying to say your mother and I and your brothers should bow down to you?" He shook his head and Joseph left, his face flushed with shame. His brothers laughed like hyenas to see their brother scolded. Only his younger brother, Benjamin, gave him a sympathetic smile. Benjamin was never cruel to him.

One morning, Joseph's older brothers were looking after their family's flock of sheep when Joseph appeared in the distance.

"Here comes the dreamer," one of them hissed.

"Now we're away from Father, let's get rid of him, once and for all. We should kill him and pretend a wild animal ate him," suggested another.

"No, let's just throw him in a pit," said Reuben, who was the eldest. He didn't love Joseph any more than the others, but he didn't want his brothers to become murderers.

When Joseph came close enough, the brothers grabbed him, tearing his beautiful coat into pieces.

Joseph screamed and struggled, but he couldn't fight them all.

"Look," said Judah, another of the brothers. He'd spotted a group of Ishmaelites in the distance. Ishmaelites were well known for slave trading. "Let's sell Joseph into slavery. Then we'll have silver coins *and* we won't have to put up with a smug and arrogant younger brother bothering us with his dreams any longer."

Joseph and the Dreams

So the brothers sold Joseph for twenty silver pieces and went home to their father. Along the way they dipped Joseph's torn coat in animal blood.

When Jacob saw it, he howled with pain. "No! Oh my son! Some wild beast must have attacked him. How did this happen?"

Before the brothers could answer, he threw himself to the ground, sobbing and tearing his own clothes in grief. "I will mourn until I join my Joseph in the grave," sobbed Jacob.

"Even now, he still loves Joseph more than any of the rest of us," thought the brothers, bitterly.

Meanwhile, Joseph was carried off to the land of Egypt, far from his home in Canaan. He was sold to a man named Potiphar, a high-ranking soldier who worked for the Pharaoh, the king of Egypt. Joseph felt terribly frightened, but he did not have to face his fear alone. God loved Joseph and watched over him.

Everything Joseph did turned out well, and the master of the house soon noticed this.

"His God grants him success," said Potiphar. "I will put him in charge of my household, so I can share in his good luck!"

Joseph found himself managing a large and wealthy house, with many slaves working for him.

He set to work and, sure enough, God smiled on Potiphar's house. But God was not the only one who was watching Joseph.

Joseph was a handsome young man, and Potiphar's wife soon took an interest in him. She called to Joseph one day when Potiphar was out. "Come here and kiss me," she demanded.

Joseph was horrified. "I can't do that. Potiphar is my master and you are his wife. It's sinful and it's wrong." He tried to get away, but the woman grabbed him by the cloak. Rushing away, his cloak tore, leaving a large piece behind.

When Potiphar came home, his wife stormed up to him. "Your slave has insulted me. He tried to kiss me! When I said no, he fought me." She held up the torn piece of cloth. "Look, he left this behind."

"How DARE he! After all I've done for him..." roared Potiphar. He summoned Joseph and began to scream at him.

"I didn't do it," said Joseph. "Please believe me."

But Potiphar was blind with rage. He had Joseph thrown into the darkest, dankest dungeon in the Pharaoh's palace.

Joseph and the Dreams

Yet Joseph still wasn't alone. God was watching over him, and He made sure that the prison guard was kind to Joseph. Before Joseph knew what was happening, he found himself in charge of all the other prisoners. "Thank you, Lord," he prayed.

A while later, the Pharaoh's baker and his butler angered the Egyptian king and he threw them in prison. The prison guard told Joseph to take them food and water every day.

When Joseph went to visit them one morning, the baker looked pale. The butler, too, seemed troubled. "Why do you look so upset?" asked Joseph. "Is something on your mind?"

The baker and the butler exchanged looks. "We both had dreams, but we do not know what they mean," the baker said at last.

Joseph and the Dreams

Joseph sat down in a corner of their cell. "Tell me your dreams," he said.

So the butler began. "In my dream I saw a grapevine. On that vine were three branches. Right before my eyes, the branches bloomed and grapes appeared and ripened. I took the grapes and squeezed them into the Pharaoh's cup, so my master could drink."

Joseph nodded, thoughtfully. "The three branches mean that in three days' time, the Pharaoh will pardon you and give you your old job back. You will be his butler once more."

The man's eyes were wide with surprise. "If this is true... then it is wonderful and you are a marvel,

Joseph! How can I repay you?"

"Please mention me to the Pharaoh," Joseph replied. "I was kidnapped and brought to this country against my will, then falsely accused. I don't deserve to be here."

"Of course!" promised the butler.

Next, the baker told his dream. He was eager for good news, just like his fellow prisoner. "I was carrying three baskets of bread," he said. "I was taking them to the Pharaoh, but birds kept eating out of the top basket. What does it mean, Joseph?"

Joseph looked at the baker with pity in his eyes. "The three baskets are three days. Within three days the Pharaoh will have you executed. I'm so sorry."

The baker shook his head. "This can't be true..."

But three days later, the Pharaoh pardoned his butler and had the baker put to death, just as Joseph had predicted.

Joseph waited patiently for the butler to tell the Pharaoh about his misfortune, but eventually he knew that the man must have forgotten him. Joseph could do nothing but pray to God, and wait.

Two years passed until, one night, the Pharaoh had a terrifying dream. He woke up with a start, sweating all over. But when he finally fell back to sleep, he dreamed again.

In the morning, he was worried. "When a man as important as I am has such dark dreams, it must mean something," he thought. So he called for the wisest men in Egypt and told them his dreams, but not one could tell him what they might mean.

Finally, the butler came to the Pharaoh, looking embarrassed. "I have just remembered something, or rather, someone who might be able to help you."

"Speak!" the Pharaoh commanded.

"When I was in prison for angering you, I met a young man from Canaan, named Joseph. He told me that my dream meant I would be released in three days. He also said that your former baker would be put to death." The butler paused. "Both those things came true."

The Pharaoh's eyes gleamed with excitement. "Well, don't just stand there, go and get him!"

Joseph was brought out from the prison, blinking

in the bright sunlight. When he had shaved and changed into clean clothes, he came before the Pharaoh.

"Tell me, Joseph, can you interpret my dreams for me? They're deeply troubling."

Joseph shook his head. "No, I cannot."

The Pharaoh turned to the butler and was about to order the guards to take him away for telling lies, when Joseph went on.

"*I* cannot interpret dreams," said Joseph. "But if you tell me what you saw, then God will tell you their meaning, through me."

The Pharaoh looked curiously at Joseph. "Well, at first I dreamed that I was standing beside the Nile when seven fat, glossy cows climbed up onto the bank. After them came seven hideous cows that were

Joseph and the Dreams

as scrawny as walking sacks of bones." The Pharaoh shuddered at the memory. "I have never seen such ugly cows in the land of Egypt. But it gets worse. The skinny, ugly cows devoured the plump and glossy cows – and even after that meal, they looked as skinny and sick as they had in the beginning."

Joseph listened carefully, nodding all the while.

The Pharaoh went on to tell Joseph his second dream. "As I fell back to sleep, I saw seven ears of corn, healthy and golden, growing on a single stalk. But then seven new ears grew, and these ones were withered and thin and scorched by the sun and the wind. The withered ears of corn ate the wholesome, healthy corn." The Pharaoh sighed. "I have told these dreams to the wisest men in the land, but no one could tell me what they might mean."

Joseph waited to be sure that the Pharaoh had finished. "Pharaoh," he said eventually, "the seven fat cows and the seven healthy ears of corn stand for seven years of plenty."

The Pharaoh clapped his hands. "That is good! Thank you, Joseph. But what about the rest?"

Joseph looked serious. "The thin, ugly cows, and the withered ears of corn mean that seven years of famine will follow the seven good years."

The Pharaoh groaned. "This is terrible."

"It doesn't have to be," said Joseph. "If you put a wise man in charge of farming in Egypt, he will make sure that you store enough food in the years of plenty to see you through the famine. With a little planning, the people need not starve."

The Pharaoh leaped to his feet and clapped Joseph

on the back. "Then we should begin today. Since God has chosen you as His messenger, surely there is no one better suited to do this job than you."

The Pharaoh pulled a beautiful ring from his finger and put it onto Joseph's own finger. "From now on, everyone will do what you say, and you will rule the kingdom for me."

Joseph bowed his head. "As you wish," he said. "And as God wishes."

The Pharaoh dressed Joseph in linen robes and hung a gold chain around his neck. They rode together in the Pharaoh's

chariot, and all of Egypt bowed down before Joseph.

For the next seven years, Joseph worked hard, day and night. He went all over Egypt, commanding farmers to store their grain. As the harvests came and went, Joseph made sure that Egypt had so many ears of corn stored up that grains of corn were almost as plentiful as grains of sand beneath the sea.

When the famine came, as Joseph had predicted, the people of Egypt cried out to the Pharaoh for food.

"Ask Joseph," the Pharaoh told them.

And when the people came to him, Joseph brought out the stored grain and everyone had enough to eat. Soon, word spread to other countries. There was famine far and wide, and people of many nations came to buy grain from Joseph.

Far away in Canaan, Joseph's father Jacob learned

that there was food in Egypt. "My sons," he said to his children, "go to Egypt and buy grain so we will not starve." He sent ten of his sons away, but he kept Benjamin with him. He couldn't bear the thought that anything might happen to his youngest boy.

When the brothers arrived in Egypt, they rushed to see Joseph. Flinging themselves on the ground before him, they begged him to sell them grain. "We have nothing," they said. "Please don't let us starve."

As they looked up at Joseph, he recognized the brothers who had sold him to the Ishmaelites all those years ago. But they did not know him. He was finely dressed and in charge of an entire kingdom, whereas the brother they remembered had been sold as a slave.

Joseph kept his expression cold and calm,

although his heart was pounding. *My brothers are bowing before me, just like the dream God sent me long ago.* "Who are you? And where are you from?" he demanded.

"We are the sons of Jacob of Canaan," said Reuben, the oldest brother. "We live there with our youngest brother, Benjamin. We did have another brother but... he's gone now." Reuben looked to the floor, his cheeks flushed with shame. The brothers looked guiltily at one another.

Joseph wondered at this. *Are they sorry for what they did?* He decided to test them. Keeping his face stern, he spoke in a resounding voice. "I suspect you to be foreign spies," he said. "I *will* sell you food, but you must bring your youngest brother, Benjamin, to me as a token of your good will. I will keep another of you here until you return." Joseph pointed to one of his brothers, named Simeon. "I'll keep him."

The brothers were afraid, and started to talk amongst themselves in their own language. They did not realize that Joseph – a foreigner in their eyes – knew what they were saying.

"This is all happening because of what we did to Joseph," said Reuben. "It's a punishment. I knew we should not treat him so badly. I should have done more to stop you."

The brothers hung their heads. "We've done a terrible thing."

Joseph had to turn away, because he was crying. "They're truly sorry," he thought. But he was still not sure if they had changed their cruel ways. "Just because they're sorry now, it doesn't mean they won't do it again," he realized, as he sent the brothers home with their grain.

They returned some time later, with Benjamin in tow, just as they had promised. Joseph welcomed them gladly, and sold them more grain. "I will release your brother Simeon. Come and have a meal with me at my house." He spoke to them all, but he was looking at Benjamin. Tears pricked his eyes. He'd missed his youngest brother very much.

As they ate, Joseph gave the boy second, third and even fourth helpings. "How is your father, is he well?" he asked the brothers.

"Very well," they replied, through mouthfuls of rich food.

Joseph was glad. He longed to see his father again, but there was one last test he needed to do to make sure that his brothers were no longer wicked men. As the brothers packed their bags to go, Joseph slipped a magnificent silver cup into Benjamin's sack.

The brothers were leaving on their donkeys when Joseph ran after them crying, "Halt! A thief has stolen my precious cup. You are the only people who have been in my house. Open your bags!"

In shock, the brothers all pulled open their sacks. Each one held only the grain and other supplies that Joseph had given them... except Benjamin's. Silver glinted amongst the corn.

Joseph snatched up the cup. "How dare you

betray my hospitality, young man!" cried Joseph.
"I will throw you in jail for your crime!"

Reuben stepped forward. "Please, sir, don't do
that. Benjamin is just an innocent boy. He cannot
have done this. I think God might be punishing us for
a terrible crime we committed years ago. Please, let
him go and take us instead. We deserve it for what we
did to our long-lost brother Joseph, who must surely
be dead by now."

With that, Joseph broke down in tears. "It's true," he sobbed. "You've really changed. Oh my brothers, I forgive you." He looked around at them, his eyes filling with tears. "I am your brother, Joseph."

Joseph held out his arms and embraced his shocked brothers, while they cried and told him how sorry they were.

"I think God meant this to happen," said Joseph. "He sent me here to save you all. For if I had not become a ruler in Egypt, I could never have given you food, and you would have starved."

So Joseph and his brothers were reunited at last. Joseph sent for his father, too. When the old man arrived in Egypt, he fell at Joseph's feet, thanking God that his son was safe.

The Pharaoh declared they should all live together

in Egypt, since their family had been apart for so long. Joseph thanked the Pharaoh, but in his heart he knew that all the thanks belonged to God, the one who had brought him to this land and given him the power to save his family.

Moses in the Rushes

In Egypt, when the pyramids gleamed, there ruled a powerful but fearful Pharaoh, who hardly trusted anyone. His greatest fear was that his kingdom would be destroyed – and he was convinced that, if it was, the people of Israel, descended from Jacob and his children, would be to blame.

"The Israelites?" asked one puzzled advisor, unable to understand why the Pharaoh was so afraid. "But they are harmless, my lord."

"*Harmless?*" scoffed the Pharaoh. "Have you seen how many of them there are? What if they were to side with our enemies? Do you think we would survive if they all turned against us?"

The court fell silent. When his advisors next spoke, it was with one voice. "What would you like us do, my lord?"

"I want the Israelites under my control," he declared. "Send my army. Have the Israelites put to work as my slaves. Then they will be powerless."

At the Pharaoh's command, a mighty army was sent out. The Israelites were rounded up and put to work, building grand temples and statues dedicated to the gods of Egypt.

The work was hard and fights often broke

out between the Israelites and their masters. They hated the way they were treated, and hated too that they were forced to build monuments celebrating the Pharaoh's power. But despite all their troubles, their numbers continued to grow.

"No matter what we do, the Israelites multiply," moaned the Pharaoh's oldest advisor. "What else can we do?"

The Pharaoh sank his face into his hands. When at last he looked up, he seemed wearier than ever. "There is only one thing left to try," he muttered, and called for his guards.

Days later, the doors to the court were flung wide and four guards entered, dragging two elderly women. At once the court was abuzz with questions. Who were these women? What could the Pharaoh be planning?

The Pharaoh raised his hand and the court settled. "Are you the midwives, who help the Israelite women give birth?" he asked.

The women nodded in unison.

"I am Shiprah, my lord," said one.

"And I am Puah," said the other.

"Then listen carefully, Shiprah and Puah," stated the Pharaoh, "for I have a task that only you and those of your profession can perform.

By your hand, every boy born to your people must be sacrificed, though every girl may keep her life. Only then will the threat of your people be ended and my mind be at peace."

The advisors gasped. The midwives were stunned. But before they could find the words to protest, the Pharaoh had his guards send the two women on their way. His decision was final.

The Pharaoh waited, looking forward to the day when he could gaze out from his palace and see the streets empty of Israelite boys. Instead, each day he woke and saw more of them – more boys – more Israelites. Angry and afraid, he summoned Shiprah and Puah again.

"We could not do as you asked, my lord," admitted Shiprah, kneeling before him. "We arrive too late. The children are born long before we get to them."

The Pharaoh was furious. He dismissed the two women without looking at them and gathered his advisors around him once more.

"Issue a decree," roared the Pharaoh, his voice shaking with

fury. "Make it known that every boy born to the Israelites is to be thrown into the river and drowned. None are to be spared."

That night, a fierce crowd of Egyptians stormed through the Israelite slums, plucking babies from their mothers' arms to find any boys.

One couple, hearing the Pharaoh's terrible command, quickly hid their newborn son. When the Egyptians burst through their door, they could not find him.

Three months passed with the boy kept safely in hiding. But his mother knew he would not stay safe for long. The Pharaoh's fears had continued to grow and the Egyptians were now searching harder than ever for Israelite boys.

Early one morning, she stole away with him to the riverside, bundled up in a basket woven out of

Moses in the Rushes

bulrushes. There she slathered the basket in slime and pitch to protect it from the water.

"Farewell, my son," she said, holding back tears as she laid the bundle down in the shallows of the river. "I dearly hope that whatever fate finds you is a better one than awaits you at home." She gave him one last fleeting smile, then covered the basket and fled. Her daughter, Miriam, stayed behind, watching over her baby brother from a distance, to see who might find him.

Later that day, the Pharaoh's daughter herself arrived at the river to wash. At once, she spotted the strange basket and had her maid bring it to her.

Carefully she peeled back the cover, and was shocked to discover...

"...A *baby?*"

At the shrillness of her voice, the baby began to cry.

"This must be one of the Israelite boys," she thought. She knew it was her duty to tell her father, but the sight of the wailing baby touched her heart. "What am I to do with you?" she wondered aloud, her voice now soft and warm.

"I can find you a nurse to take care of him, if you would like."

Startled, the Pharaoh's daughter turned to find Miriam, looking up at her nervously.

"Yes..." decided the Pharaoh's daughter, pushing her father's orders far from her mind. "Go at once and find a nurse to raise this child."

Miriam ran away, smiling with relief. When she returned, it was her mother who followed sheepishly behind.

The Pharaoh's daughter handed over the baby, unaware that she was returning him to his real mother. "His name is Moses," she said with a smile. "I drew him from the water. Raise him well."

And she did. Moses grew up strong and good, protected from the deadly decree by the kindness of the Pharaoh's own daughter.

Eventually, Moses outgrew the need for a nurse. His mother took him to the palace where she said her goodbyes for the second time. Then the Pharaoh's daughter welcomed him inside, dressed him in fine clothes, and led him to the court of her father – now an old man.

"Who is this?" asked the Pharaoh, confused and

intrigued by a boy he had every right to fear.

"This is Moses," announced the Pharaoh's daughter. "My son – your grandson – and the newest member of our royal family."

Moses and the Burning Bush

Moses and the Burning Bush

For many years, Moses had been living the life of a prince of Egypt, kept from the everyday struggles and hardships of most people. But Moses carried a dangerous secret. He hadn't been born to this life. He was born an Israelite – a hated slave of the Egyptians.

Moses had been adopted into the royal family, with his past kept hidden from the Pharaoh. He had always been careful not to let the truth slip out. Until, one day, he spied an Egyptian beating an Israelite worker.

"No, stop!" he yelled, sprinting to reach the Egyptian. "I command you to stop!"

But his cry came too late. With a final, terrible blow, the worker fell to the floor, dead.

Moses stared in shock at the fallen worker – an Israelite, like himself. A powerful rage stirred in him. Grasping his staff, he stormed over to the Egyptian. There was a short struggle, but only one man stood at the end of it.

"What have I done?" gasped Moses, looking down in horror. "I... I've killed him."

It wasn't long before the Pharaoh discovered Moses' crime. He sent for the prince, but when the Pharaoh's guards entered his room, they found it empty. Moses had fled.

Years went by, and soon almost everyone had forgotten about Moses. Nobody knew where he had disappeared to, though some said that he was living as a beggar on the streets.

The truth was, Moses had left Egypt altogether. He had made it to the land of Midian, where he had met and married a beautiful woman named Zipporah. Now he worked as a shepherd for her father, Jethro, and had never been happier.

"Where do you think you're going?" Moses called, one warm summer morning. The sky was clear, the air was fresh, and the sheep were grazing peacefully all around him.

"Yes, I'm talking to you," he continued, his eyes fixed on a lamb that was leaping up the slopes to Mount Horeb.

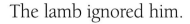

The lamb ignored him.

With a sigh, Moses chased after it, hoping to catch it before it got into any trouble. But when he arrived at the foot of the mountain, the lamb stopped in its tracks. So too did Moses, for in front of him was a bush, burning with the most intense flames he had ever seen.

"I don't understand," said Moses. "The fire looks so fierce, but the bush remains unharmed."

"Moses," whispered the Burning Bush, and Moses fell back with a cry of alarm.

"Moses," the bush went on, "remove your sandals, for this is holy ground."

Poor Moses had no idea what was happening. But the strangeness of it all had him rooted to the spot – too much in awe to run away. He slid off his sandals, bowed his head and listened.

"I am the God of your father, and his father before him. I have seen how your people suffer under the cruel rule of the Egyptians. And by your hands, I will see it ended."

"M... mine?" spluttered Moses.

"Yes, Moses. You will lead My people free of Egypt, to a land flowing with milk and honey."

Moses couldn't believe it. "Who am I to save the Israelites?" he demanded. "Even if I returned to them, they would mock me and ask me who sent me, and what would I say then?"

"I AM THAT I AM," boomed the Burning Bush,

spitting sparks into the air. "You will say I AM has sent you, and they will know Me."

But Moses clung to his doubts. "They won't believe me. How could they? How will they know that You have really talked to me?"

When the Bush next spoke, it was with a voice more gentle than a breeze. "The staff in your hand. Throw it down."

Moses did as he was told and at once the staff became a serpent. It slithered along the ground at his feet.

"What miracle is this?" cried Moses, wide-eyed. As he stared, the Bush issued its next order.

"Reach out your hand, Moses, and take it by the tail."

Slowly – very slowly – Moses reached out. He

Moses and the Burning Bush

hesitated a moment, then grabbed the serpent by the tail. And with that it became a staff again.

"Return to Egypt. Take your staff and use it to do wonders in My name. Through them all will know Me and all will believe."

"But I am no speaker, Lord. I am bad with words. I cannot do as You ask."

The Bush grew angry again, and the flames turned blue and blazed so brightly that Moses was forced to look away. "Find your brother, Aaron the Levite, first son of your Hebrew mother. He will be your voice, as I will be your power, and together you will set My people free. Now go, Moses. Waste no more time here." With these final words, the fire faded as if it had never been.

Moses walked away from Mount Horeb in a daze.

The sky was clear, the air was fresh, and the sheep were still quietly grazing as though nothing unusual had happened.

"Set my people free..." Moses whispered, reliving his encounter with the Burning Bush. He took a long, deep breath before releasing it in a shuddering sigh.

It was time to return to Egypt.

Moses and the Plagues

On his throne in Egypt, the Pharaoh was in hysterics. "Did you hear that?" he asked his advisors between fits of laughter. He pointed to the pair of scruffy men who had so rudely demanded audience before his court. "'Let the Israelites go free,' they said. Can you believe it?"

Some of the Pharaoh's advisors shook their heads, while others chuckled along with him. The Israelites were the Egyptians' slaves. They were excellent workers, so the very idea of giving them their freedom was more than funny –

it was ridiculous.

"Well?" the Pharaoh snorted, trying to keep a straight face. "Who are you to demand anything of a Pharaoh?"

"I am Aaron," said the first of the men, "and this is my brother, Moses, messenger of God."

At the mention of his name, a chorus of muttering filled the court. Moses shrank back, clutching his staff so hard that his knuckles turned white.

The Pharaoh was intrigued. "Moses...?" he said, sitting up in his throne. "The impostor?" He had not been Pharaoh when Moses was a boy, but he knew all about the Israelite who, for a time, had lived in the palace as an Egyptian prince. "What foolishness is this? Moses hasn't been seen in years. He is dead or else long gone."

Moses and the Plagues

Now, Moses had achieved much since the Burning Bush had told him to return to Egypt. He had been reunited with his brother, Aaron, and had convinced the Israelites that, with God on his side, he would lead them to freedom. All he had to do now was keep that promise.

Moses cleared his throat. "I *am* Moses," he declared. "And on behalf of God, I demand that you let my people go."

This time the whole court burst into laughter. Dead man, impostor, messenger for the Hebrew God – whoever this man was, he was quite clearly crazy.

Moses fell quiet, but Aaron had not finished. He snatched the staff from Moses' hand and hurled it to the floor with a clatter. It lay there for a while, unmoving. Then, to the amazement of the court, the hard wood bent and writhed, transforming into soft, scaly flesh. Sharp fangs erupted from one end, and where a staff had been, now slithered a great serpent.

The Pharaoh was unimpressed. "Is that the best your God can do for you?" With a waft of his hand, two cloaked figures emerged from the shadows, each carrying a staff. "My magicians can do so much better."

The magicians threw their staffs to the floor. There was a flash of light and they too became serpents. But just as quickly as they were made, Moses' staff swallowed each serpent whole.

"Tricks, nothing but tricks!"

the Pharaoh growled, all traces of laughter gone. "Your God has no real power and I will not free your people. Now leave my sight." And he called for his guards to drag them out.

But the next morning, when the Pharaoh was lounging on his royal barge, Moses and Aaron appeared on the nearby shore.

"Pharaoh!" announced Aaron. "I speak for Moses and for God when I say to you: let my people go."

The Pharaoh sighed. "And what will you do if I refuse? More games with sticks and snakes?"

Rather than reply, Aaron waded out into the river until the water came up to his knees. He raised his staff high over his head, then plunged it firmly into the water.

At first, nothing happened. All those aboard the

barge giggled and guffawed. But they soon fell silent when, moments later, the water around Aaron grew dark and murky. In an instant, the darkness spread and the entire river turned to blood.

"Just another trick," declared the Pharaoh. He snapped his fingers and his magicians appeared beside him. "Show them how it's done."

The magicians brought out a bowl of clean water. They waved their hands over it, made click-clacking noises with their tongues, and that water too turned blood red.

"See! Your God has no real power," shouted the Pharaoh triumphantly. "I am Pharaoh. I do not fear your God and I will not let your people go. Sail on!"

Moses and the Plagues

For many weeks, Moses and Aaron continued to pursue the Pharaoh, demanding he free the Israelites. And now, each time the Pharaoh refused, a terrible plague was unleashed upon Egypt.

First came a plague of frogs that swarmed through the streets. They hopped into houses, bathed in drinking water, and chased people around the city.

The Pharaoh's magicians were powerless. They could make more frogs, but they couldn't get rid of them. Eventually the constant croaking became too much for the Pharaoh.

"Fine," he agreed. "Rid me of these pests. Then you can take your people and go."

But when the frogs were gone, the Pharaoh

broke his promise with a smile: "The frogs have left. I see no reason to give up the Israelites."

So God sent lice and then biting flies to make life uncomfortable – and itchy – for the Egyptians and their animals. Again, the magicians were unable to stop them, and again the Pharaoh promised to give in. But the moment the plagues were ended, he went back on his word.

"Things will only get worse," warned Aaron. "Your cattle will die, and your skin will be covered with boils and oozing sores. Please, let our people go."

"I will do no such thing" answered the Pharaoh. "Do your worst, Israelites."

And they did.

As threatened, the cattle of the Egyptians dropped dead where they stood and, soon after, every Egyptian man, woman and child broke out in painful boils and sores. But the Pharaoh would not relent.

Days after his sores had healed, the Pharaoh was sitting on his throne when an advisor burst in, shrieking: "Fire! Fire! The sky is raining fire!"

The Pharaoh went out onto his balcony and, sure enough, fire was raining down from the sky. One large fireball missed him by a hand's width, and when it landed it exploded into shards of ice.

"What sorcery is this?" thought the Pharaoh.

As if in reply, the Pharaoh heard his name being called from the courtyard below. He looked down to find Moses standing unharmed amidst the chaos.

"I ask you again. Let my people go!"

The Pharaoh flinched as another fireball struck the palace – and another. For as far as the Pharaoh could

Moses and the Plagues

see, the sky was ablaze with fiery hail, while down below his city was burning.

"Take them," he shouted, above the noise of screaming advisors and exploding hail. "I give in. Just stop this madness and leave."

But after the hail ended and the fires were put out, the Pharaoh would not let the Israelites go.

Even when a plague of locusts devoured the crops in Egypt – or when Moses lifted his hands to the sky and stole all light from the land for three days – the Pharaoh would not give in.

"I've survived your plagues, and I will continue to do so," he declared. "There is nothing more you can throw at me."

"Please," Moses replied. "What comes next is more terrible than you can imagine. I ask once more, for your sake: let my people go."

"No, Moses," spat the Pharaoh. "I am Pharaoh and my word is final. I will not let your people go."

"So be it," whispered Moses, and he left the Pharaoh alone in the dark.

In the days that followed, Moses and Aaron went among the Israelites, telling each household to take a lamb and sacrifice it to God, using its blood to mark the doorway of their house.

It was at midnight, when all the Israelites were safe inside their homes and all their doorways had been marked, that God released his final plague on Egypt.

A gentle breeze stirred through the streets. That was how it started. Then, like a living thing, it grew stronger... Bolder... It moved from house to house, slipping through doorways and windows – but always passing over Israelite homes.

The wind visited every Egyptian house all the way
to the Pharaoh's palace, which it entered last of all
before fading to nothing. And with its passing, a great
cry resounded through Egypt.

Moses walked through the city with a heavy heart,
past buildings alive with the shrieks and howls of
suffering families. When he arrived at the palace, he
found the lights were out – and there, in the shadows,
was the Pharaoh on his throne, his eldest son dead
in his arms.

Hearing Moses enter, the Pharaoh's head whipped up like a viper. "What have you done?" he hissed.

"I warned you, Pharaoh. You had the chance to stop this. You could have let my people go. You could have believed in the power of my God. Now He has taken the lives of all Egyptian firstborn children. Including your son."

The Pharaoh glowered at Moses, his eyes full of hatred. He opened his mouth, and for a second Moses was sure he would shout or yell or curse his name. Instead, the Pharaoh's eyes returned to his son. "Take them..." he whispered. "Take your people and get out." And he said nothing more.

Moses hastened to tell the Israelites of the Pharaoh's decision, urging them to pack fast and leave. With God on their side, the Israelites had been given their freedom. But all knew how quickly a Pharaoh could change his mind...

Moses and the Red Sea

"Are we nearly there yet?" asked Moses' youngest son, Eliezer, fixing his father with hopeful eyes.

Moses shook his head. "We still have a long way to go before we arrive in the Land of the Canaanites – the land promised to us by God."

Eliezer sighed. It felt as though they had been walking forever. He looked around at the hundreds of thousands of Israelites, rescued from slavery by his father and his uncle, Aaron. There were so many of them, he could hardly see anything else.

"Isn't there a quicker way?" he asked.

Now it was Moses' turn to sigh. He stopped walking and pointed to the distance, where Eliezer could just make out a pillar of cloud, bridging the sky and the land. "We follow that pillar of cloud by day, and by night we follow a pillar of fire. They guide us where God wills us to go – so there is no other way."

What Moses didn't say was that the quicker way would lead them through the land of the Philistines – a place of war and violence that might frighten the Israelites into returning to Egypt.

"Aren't you scared?" said Eliezer.

"Scared? Of what?"

"The Pharaoh, back in Egypt," Eliezer replied. "Scared he'll change his mind and come after us."

Moses laughed and patted his son on the back.

"Do not worry, my son. Whatever happens, God will be with us." And they continued walking.

It was only later, after making it to the land of Etham, that Moses learned his son's fears had come true. The sky was dark, the Israelites were resting, and in the distance the pillar of fire was blazing brightly.

"Moses," came God's voice.

Moses' eyes flew open.

"The Pharaoh is coming, Moses. I have hardened his heart and stirred him to action. I made him rally his troops. 'We were fools to let the Israelites go,' he shouted at them. 'We must set out to reclaim what we have lost.' So he pursues you, Moses, with all his captains and all his chariots behind him."

Moses felt his heart sink. His hands were clammy, his brow was beaded with sweat... "Lord, why would you do such a thing?" he demanded.

"So that all will know Me," replied God. "And that all will know of My power. But fear not, Moses. Put your trust in Me. Lead My people to the Red Sea and there I will make My stand."

Moses did as God commanded. The Israelites followed him to the Red Sea, where they set up camp.

"Why are we stopping here, Father?" asked Eliezer. "There's no way ahead – no bridge or boat large enough to take us all across."

But Moses was too busy staring behind them to reply. Eliezer followed his gaze and saw a cloud of rising dust on the horizon. "What's that?"

"Not what," muttered Moses, "but who." He turned to his son and with a voice heavy with guilt said: "The Pharaoh is riding this way."

Eliezer gasped. So did his mother and his older brother, Gershom. The bad news quickly spread from person to person until soon Moses found himself at the mercy of an angry crowd.

"I knew this was a mistake!" shouted one furious Israelite. "You have led us to our deaths out here."

"We should never have left Egypt," yelled another.

Moses tried his best to calm his people, explaining that God would fight for them. Some listened and prayed, but many more ignored him and continued to shout and cry. Meanwhile, the dust cloud grew larger, and eventually people could make out the shapes of chariots and the glint of sun on polished metal.

"Father, what are we to do?" cried Eliezer.

At that moment, the pillar of cloud that had led the Israelites on their journey descended in front of the Egyptians, where it became a cloud of darkness, hiding the way ahead and slowing their pursuit. God was protecting the Israelites.

"Moses," whispered God, "the darkness will not hold them for long. Listen carefully and do exactly as I say..."

Following God's instructions, Moses approached the edge of the Red Sea. He raised his staff to the sky and at once a gust of wind burst forth, distracting the Israelites from their panic and causing Moses' robes to billow wildly around him. Then, with a gesture, he called the wind down upon the water, where it blew with the force of a hurricane – powerful enough to push the water whichever way he pleased. At his command, the wind separated the water into two halves, clearing a path of sea floor between them.

"Come!" he shouted above the howling wind. "We have a way across. Now we must hurry along it."

The Israelites were stupefied by what Moses had just done, but with the Egyptians closing in, they wasted no time following him through the Red Sea.

The journey across the sea floor was long and difficult. It was also full of wonder, with children and adults alike pausing to gape at the strange silhouettes of sea creatures swimming in the watery walls.

Their amazement turned to dread when they saw the Egyptians emerge from the cloud of darkness and speed after them through the parted sea.

"Do not be afraid," Moses shouted to his people. "God is on our side." And with those words, the pillar of fire set upon the chariots, taking off their wheels and sending them swerving out of control.

Moses and the Red Sea

"Now, Moses. End this," whispered God.

Moses spread his hand to the sky and the Israelites felt the wind drop. Then came a rumble, followed by a thunderous crash of water and a terrible chorus of shrieks. Behind them, the walls of sea were collapsing in huge torrents, washing away the Pharaoh and all who followed him.

The Israelites cried out with joy. Their pursuers were defeated. As they reached the opposite shore, they sang and cheered and gave thanks to God. Just as God had planned, His people now believed and all knew of His might.

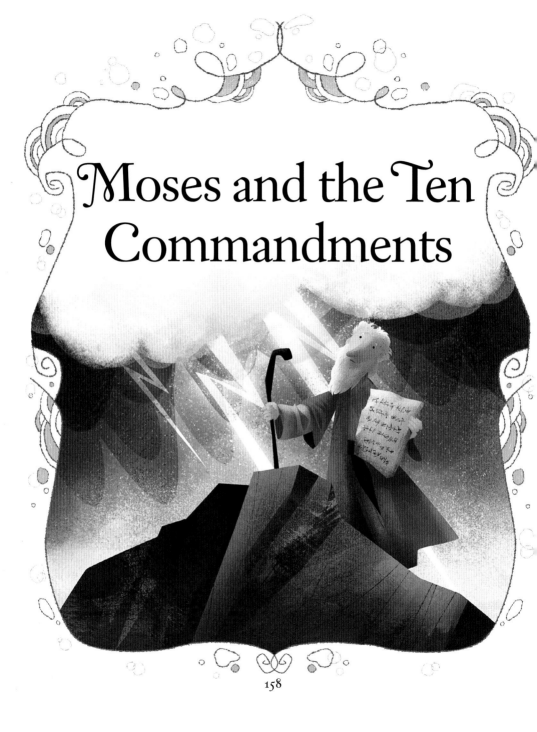

Moses and the Ten Commandments

As dusk faded to night, Moses walked back to his tent. It had been another long, tiring day solving the disputes of his people, and he still had much to do.

In fact, Moses was so distracted by the tasks before him that he failed to notice the sound of heavy footsteps approaching from behind...

"My son!" boomed a deep, gruff voice.

Startled, Moses barely managed to turn around before the breath was squeezed out of him by the embrace of a man twice his size.

When the man let go, Moses stumbled back

with a splutter. "Jethro!" he gasped, drawing precious air back into his lungs. "How is this–? What brings you–? I haven't seen you since..."

"Since you left Midian with my daughter and my grandchildren? Since before you freed the Israelites and led them out of Egypt, through the Red Sea, and off in search of a land promised to you by God? You certainly have been busy, haven't you, Moses?" Jethro let out a mighty laugh. But when he saw the troubled look on Moses' face, his cheerfulness dwindled. "Are you not happy to see your father-in-law?"

Moses tried his best to smile, but it was no use. "I'm sorry, Jethro. We've been through so much, I have grown weary. Come, let us eat and offer up our thanks to God. Then I will explain everything."

Jethro and Moses stayed up late into the night,

eating, drinking and discussing all that had happened since the Israelites had left Egypt.

"...and then, in Rephidim, we fought Amalek and his men," said Moses. "I held my staff up throughout the battle, which granted God's power to my people and led to our victory. But the battle was long, and the effort drained me. And now, each day – all day – my people come to me seeking my counsel. And I am so tired..."

Jethro took a good look at his dear son-in-law and noticed how Moses' skin sagged, and how heavy his eyelids looked, falling low over bloodshot eyes.

"No wonder my daughter sent for me," said Jethro, shaking his head. "The burden you carry is too great for one man. It will wear you down."

"But what else can I do?" asked Moses.

Jethro thought long and hard. "You must share the responsibility, Moses. Teach your people God's laws and have them decide for themselves how best to live their lives."

It was wise advice, and Moses was quick to follow it. He divided the Israelites into groups, each one governed by an able man, chosen and then educated by Moses in the laws of God. But while his burden was lessened, Moses still found himself being called upon day and night for his wisdom.

All too soon, Jethro had to return home and Moses led his people on. By the time the Israelites arrived at the foot of Mount Sinai, Moses was exhausted. But before he had the chance to rest, he heard the voice of God whispering in his ear, urging him up the mountainside.

"What do you want from me, Lord?" sighed Moses as he staggered up the steep slopes.

"I bring good news for you and the children of Israel," announced God, as Moses reached the summit. "Tell everyone to prepare themselves – to wash their clothes and be ready – for three days from now I shall come down here, in sight of everyone."

"You'll do what?" asked Moses, more than a little surprised.

"I will show Myself, Moses. But let it be known that none may touch the mountain or climb its slopes but you."

Back at camp, Moses explained to the people all that God had said. Excited, they set to work, doing what God had asked of them while eagerly awaiting His arrival.

And what an arrival it was.

On the third day, a thick, dark cloud swallowed the mountain's summit, booming and crackling with thunder and lightning. Shocked, the Israelites jumped as one when a harsh trumpet blared. Then they trembled, cried out and clutched each other as God descended in a blaze of fire, setting the Earth to quaking beneath their feet.

Nobody spoke. Nobody could speak, for they had no words for what they were seeing. Alone, Moses made his way up the mountainside, through the dark clouds, to where God waited in all His glory.

"I am the Lord your God," declared God between the rumbles of thunder, "and you shall have no other gods but Me. This is My first commandment." With His first commandment spoken, God continued to

Moses and the Ten Commandments

list nine more, each as important as the last:

"When you speak My name, say it with respect.

Work for six days and keep the seventh as a holy day of rest.

Do not make images or objects to worship.

Always respect your mother and your father.

Do not kill any human being.

Husbands and wives must be faithful.

Do not steal.

Do not tell lies.

Do not be envious of the things others have."

These were the laws that Moses and his people were to follow without question – laws that were to last long after Moses was gone.

"Now go, Moses. Tell My people all you have heard, then return to Me, for I have much still to say."

Moses did as God asked, and the people praised God and made sacrifices to Him for the gift of His commandments.

The next time Moses went up the mountain, he seemed to stay up there for a very long time indeed...

"It's been weeks!" moaned an old, toothless woman. "Where's Moses? Where is he? Without him, how are we to reach the Promised Land – the land flowing with milk and honey, promised to us by God? Who will settle our disputes and remind us of God's laws? Who will–"

With Moses gone, the Israelites had quickly fallen prey to panic and doubt, and Aaron, Moses' brother, had grown tired of their bickering.

"Enough," he declared, interrupting the old woman's rant. "Moses will return. Have faith."

"So you keep saying," rasped the old woman, "but that doesn't help us now. Give us something we can see, something to believe in. Show us the God that freed us from Egypt."

Aaron pondered this. Then, in one quick motion, he swiped a gold earring free from the woman's drooping earlobe. Ignoring her outraged shrieks, he demanded: "Bring me the gold earrings of your husbands, your children and your wives, and I shall give you your God."

The people did as Aaron asked. He took the earrings and melted them down, and from that metal he created a gleaming golden calf for them to worship.

Days later, Moses staggered down the slopes of Mount Sinai, clutching two stone tablets tightly to his chest. God had taught Moses much in their time together on the summit, but the tablets were His greatest gift, inscribed by His hand with the ten commandments.

As Moses reached the edge of the camp, he heard music and chanting. He went on until he met with a vast circle of dancing Israelites. And there, deep in the middle of them, he spied a glimmer of gold...

"You fools!" he roared, cutting through the sound of merriment.

In stunned silence, everyone turned to face Moses, just as the old man hurled the stone tablets to the ground, where they shattered into pieces.

"What was that? What have you done?" asked Aaron.

"It is not what I have done, but what you have done. Fools, every single one of you!" replied Moses. He charged through the camp, wrenched the golden calf from its shrine and threw it into the fire.

"I have not been gone more than forty days, and in that time you have broken the first of God's commandments in your worship of this false god! You are not worthy of His laws, which lie shattered on the ground, as broken as your promises."

Appalled, Aaron realized his terrible mistake. He went straight to Moses, full of regret and seeking forgiveness.

Moses knew Aaron was a good man. So when he ordered his closest followers to go through the camp, killing all those loyal to the calf, Aaron was spared.

When the killing was at an end and the calf was

no more than a molten lump, Moses returned to his tent to consider his people's crime. He knew they had done great wrong, but without the tablets to remind them of God's laws, they would only continue to sin.

And so, in time, God wrote new stone tablets and Moses stored them in a golden box – known as the Ark of the Covenant – so that the people could take God's laws wherever they went.

Once the tablets were safely stored away, Moses let out a heavy sigh. His bones ached and his trembling fingers clutched tightly to his staff. Age was catching up with him. But with the tablets to guide them, he knew his people would remain true to God's ways until they reached the Promised Land – however long that might take...

Joshua and the Battle of Jericho

Joshua and the Battle of Jericho

"God has spoken to me and He is still on our side!" Joshua declared, grabbing the edge of the table in his makeshift headquarters. His generals exchanged excited glances. This was the news they had been waiting to hear ever since Joshua had become their leader after the death of Moses.

"We've been wandering around in the wilderness now for forty years," Joshua continued. "The time has come to make a home for ourselves. To take what's rightfully ours – what God promised us: the land of Canaan!"

Joshua and the Battle of Jericho

It was stirring stuff, and Joshua's generals were right to be excited. The great Israelite leader and prophet Moses had defeated the Egyptians and freed the Israelites from slavery nearly half a century earlier. God had promised his people a refuge in Canaan – a land flowing with milk and honey and, they hoped, other good things too; a place of plenty where they could put down their roots. But, since then, things had gone badly wrong. Many of the Israelites, afraid of the difficulties that lay ahead, and not trusting God to help them defeat the Canaanites, had refused to invade Canaan as God had commanded. As a punishment, they had been condemned to roam the wilderness.

But now, at last, the Israelites were camped on the banks of the River Jordan. On the opposite side lay the great Canaanite city of Jericho. They were convinced that if they could only destroy Jericho, then the land of Canaan would be theirs for the taking. But it was a very big 'if'. Jericho was well-fortified and wouldn't be easy to conquer. It was going to take a lot of careful planning.

So Joshua sent two of his most trusted men into the city to spy for him. Their mission – to find out everything there was to know about Jericho.

Pretending to be merchants, the spies easily entered the city and set about shadowing the city guards. They soon found out when and where the city's forces went on duty, what sorts of weapons they used, and how they protected themselves in battle. They discovered how thick and high the town walls were. They hung around the markets and taverns, eavesdropping and chatting with the locals to see how popular the king was. And they discreetly asked around to discover how much food and water there was in the city.

Every night, they went back to their lodgings in a seedy part of town, where they were staying with a woman named Rahab. She had agreed to let them stay with her as long as they, in turn, promised to spare her family when the Israelites attacked.

"Everyone here is terrified of you Israelites," she told them, "ever since you defeated the Egyptians all those years ago. If your army can get into the city, they won't meet much resistance." Defeating Jericho would be child's play, she assured them.

It took only a few days for the spies to gather all the information they needed. As they left, they told

Rahab how to protect her family when the Israelites invaded. "Decorate your house with red ribbons," one told her. "That way, it will stand out from the other houses and we'll know not to attack it." Rahab, listening carefully, nodded. "And make sure you stay indoors," the other added. Then they said their goodbyes and headed back across the river to the Israelites' camp.

Soon Joshua knew all he needed to know. He knew Jericho's secrets and weaknesses, but he also knew its strengths. Jericho was indeed a formidable city. The people might be afraid of the Israelites, but they were well equipped to defend themselves against attack. How could the Israelites ever succeed?

One night while Joshua was strolling around the camp, he saw a stranger with a drawn sword.

"Who are you? A friend or an enemy?" Joshua called out.

"Neither," replied the stranger, his voice booming. It echoed so loudly around the camp that it shook the tents themselves. "I am the commander of the Lord's army."

Immediately, Joshua flung himself on the ground.

"Wh... what do you want me to do?" Joshua stuttered, for although he was a brave man, this was, after all, a messenger from God.

"Take off your sandals. You are on holy ground," the man demanded.

Quickly, Joshua did as he was told,

not daring to look at the man.

"I will help you to destroy Jericho," the commander bellowed. "All you have to do is this..."

The next day, Joshua gathered together the high priests of the Israelites, and told them to lift up the Ark of the Covenant, a box that held the sacred Ten Commandments that God had given to Moses. "I want you to march around the city with an armed guard," he ordered. "And I want seven of you to walk before the Ark, blowing trumpets."

The priests thought it a bizarre request, but they did as they were told.

Then Joshua addressed his army: "Men, I want you to hold your heads high and your weapons aloft, and march proudly behind the Ark as the priests carry it around the city. But whatever you do, don't say a word. Don't give out any war cries. And absolutely no shouting until I give you the order to shout. Then, you must shout as if your lives depend on it!"

It took a while to get everyone organized, but by late afternoon, the procession was in full-flow: a troop of guards at the front, the chief priests with the Ark of the Covenant next, and the army bringing up the rear. The people of Jericho hid behind their solid city walls, waiting fearfully and wondering what was

happening. *What were the Israelites up to?*

By the time the priests and soldiers had gone all the way around the city once, it was almost evening, so they made camp outside the city walls. They were going to need a good night's sleep, as Joshua wanted them to repeat the performance the next day.

And the next.

And the one after that...

In fact, this went on for six days. It was tiring work, and the Israelites had no idea what Joshua was

planning, but still they did as he commanded. They had already learned the hard way that disobedience was a bad idea. Meanwhile, as each day passed, the people of Jericho became more and more afraid.

On the seventh day, the soldiers and priests rose at daybreak. Joshua had told them that today they were to march around the city seven times. Undaunted, they set off, sensing that something extraordinary was about to happen. They were right. As they finished the seventh lap, and the priests blew their trumpets, Joshua cried out, "Now, shout! Shout as loudly as you can!"

The trumpets sounded again and the men yelled at the top of their voices, until their lungs ached and their throats hurt, and the mighty walls of Jericho came crashing to the ground.

Joshua and the Battle of Jericho

The Israelites were astonished, but quickly gathered their wits, and rushed into the city. They killed everyone and everything in sight – only Rahab and those in her house were spared.

Ransacking the city, they took all the gold and silver and precious metals to offer up to God, and then they burned down what was left. And to be completely sure that Jericho could never be used by the Canaanites again, Joshua placed a curse on it.

"Cursed be anyone who tries to rebuild this city!" he shouted. "At the cost of his firstborn son will he lay its foundations; at the cost of his youngest will he set up its gates."

With Jericho utterly destroyed, Joshua knew that the Canaanites would be filled with terror. After all, if the Israelites could destroy Jericho, then surely nothing could stop them. More importantly, the Israelites had proved that they had God on their side.

And *that* made them invincible.

The Story
of Samson

The Story of Samson

Samson the Israelite was no ordinary man, standing a full head taller than anyone alive, with broad shoulders and rippling muscles. A huge mane of curly hair tumbled from his head down to his waist. It had never been cut – a sign of his devotion to God.

Samson had chosen himself a beautiful bride, from a group of people known as the Philistines. The Philistines were the sworn enemies of the Israelites – but Samson didn't care.

The Story of Samson

One day, on the way to meet his bride-to-be, Samson was attacked by a lion. Samson swatted the beast to the ground. With his bare hands, he wrenched open the lion's jaws and ripped the whole animal in half. Shocked at his own strength, Samson stumbled into town, but didn't tell anyone what had happened.

As he headed home, Samson walked past the dead lion and noticed a swarm of bees making a hive inside its body. Ever unafraid, he reached in and scooped out a handful of delicious honey.

A month later, Samson returned for his wedding day. There were thirty guests at the wedding, all Philistines. After a huge feast, the guests challenged each other to solve riddles. This was a game Samson loved. Eager to win, he made a bet.

"If any of you can solve this riddle, I'll buy each of you a fine new set of clothes. Here's my riddle: *Out of the eater, something to eat. And out of the strong, something sweet.* I'll give you seven days to find the answer."

Certain that no one could solve his riddle, Samson went to his new home with his wife. Sure enough, after six days no one had managed to come up with a solution.

That night, Samson's wife whispered in his ear. "Well done, husband. You're going to win that bet, I know it! But please, won't you tell *me* the answer?"

"Of course," said Samson, grinning broadly. "The

answer is 'a lion'. You see, a month ago I killed a lion – an eater and something strong – and then later I found some bees inside its body, making honey – something sweet to eat."

Samson fell into a deep, satisfied sleep. He didn't notice his wife get out of bed, dress and sneak off to her brothers' house, to tell them the solution.

The next morning, when all thirty wedding guests appeared at his house with the right answer, Samson flew into a fury. He stormed off to a nearby Philistine town, killed thirty men, and gave their clothes to the guests from his wedding. "And I never want to see you again!" he roared at his wife, knowing that she must have betrayed him.

The Philistines wanted revenge, but were terrified of Samson's great strength. It was some years later that they came up with a trick. They formed an army and surrounded a town of Israelites far from Samson's home.

"Why are you suddenly attacking us now?" called out the town leader.

"We won't hurt you," the Philistine leader began, "*if* we can take revenge on Samson. Bring him to us, and we'll leave."

They allowed a messenger to scurry across the hills to Samson's town. "Please, mighty Samson," begged the messenger, "we need your help. Our town is under siege from the Philistines. They want us to bring you to them."

"Dead?" asked Samson.

"No, but we do have to tie you up."

Samson thought about it, and prayed to God. He

was sure God would keep him safe, so he agreed.

With his enormous arms tied behind his back in thick ropes, Samson made his way to the Philistine camp. A soldier pressed the tip of his spear onto Samson's back, forcing him to walk out into the desert. After a long walk, they stopped on top of a mound littered with the bones of dead animals.

Samson turned around to see not just that one soldier but an army of hundreds facing him, all gripping spears. At that moment, he felt a great heat flow through the ground and into his body. His muscles burned red hot, and he flexed them with such ferocity that the ropes snapped. Samson snarled, grabbed a bone from the ground, and tore into the Philistine army.

Some hours later, Samson groaned and collapsed

The Story of Samson

in exhaustion. He had killed every single man who had come to attack him – nearly a thousand in all. He was hot, tired, and desperately thirsty. "O God!" he shouted up at the sky. "You gave me the strength to destroy my enemies. But what will You do with me now? Will You let me die of thirst out here in the desert?"

God answered Samson by making the earth beneath his feet tremble. The ground split open, and a spring of water gushed from it.

When the Israelites heard about Samson's miraculous victory, and God's blessing on him, they agreed to make him their leader. Samson kept the Israelites safe for twenty years, but he could not keep himself out of trouble.

Once, he wandered into a town called Gaza. He ate and drank so much that he fell asleep before he could leave, collapsing beside the massive town gate. A Philistine spy had been watching. He persuaded the people of Gaza to help him tie Samson to the gate, thinking that he would be trapped.

When Samson woke up, he couldn't move his arms. So he stood up, lifting the entire gate onto his back. He carried it all the way home, where the Israelites cut him loose.

Samson's final undoing came when he fell in love with a woman named Delilah and wanted to get married again.

Delilah, however, was not in love with Samson.

The Story of Samson

She was happy to marry him because he was a mighty leader, but what she really cared about was money. And so, when a conspiracy of Philistine lords offered to pay her eleven hundred pieces of silver to betray her husband, she agreed.

"Samson has always been able to defeat our soldiers because of his great strength," explained the lords. "You must find out the secret of his strength, and tell us."

That evening, Delilah talked sweetly to Samson. "I'm curious, husband... You're so strong, no one has ever been able to hold you prisoner. What would someone have to do to keep you tied up?"

Samson, remembering how his first wife had betrayed him, was not prepared to give up his secret. So he told a lie.

"Why, it's simple," he replied. "Whoever wanted to bind me would have to use a new bowstring, one that has never fired an arrow."

The very next day, Delilah bought some new bowstrings, waited until Samson was asleep, and tied him up. She called the Philistines to the house – then quickly woke Samson. "Samson, Samson, the Philistines are coming. You'd better run!"

Samson sat up and rubbed his eyes. He had snapped the bowstrings without even noticing they were there. Seeing this through the window, the Philistines ran away.

That night, Delilah pretended to be annoyed. "Samson, you lied to me! I tried tying you up with brand new bowstrings while you were asleep, but you snapped the knots as if they weren't there."

"Did I say *bowstrings*?" asked Samson. "I meant to say, *ropes*. A good, thick and newly-made rope is the secret to keeping me tied up." But Samson was still telling a lie, and when Delilah tied him up that night with a new set of ropes, he snapped them easily too.

"Stop teasing me, Samson," Delilah complained. There must be something I can tie you up with that you can't break out of."

"Well, in fact, there is one thing you can do," said Samson. "The secret is my hair. If you tie my hair up with a set of pins, so that it's all wrapped up in a knot on top of my head, then I will be as weak as a lamb."

Once again, Delilah waited until Samson had fallen asleep, and followed his instructions. Once again, she summoned the Philistines to her house, this time sure Samson had told her the truth.

"Quick, Samson, wake up!" Delilah cried out. "The Philistines are here!"

"Why must you play these games when the Philistines are nearby?" groaned Samson, jolting awake. He pulled the pins out of his hair and lumbered up to the window, leering and scowling at the Philistines gathered outside.

"Why must *you* keep lying to me, husband!" Delilah shrieked back. "Haven't I always woken you up in plenty of time? Do you really think I'd let those brutes harm you?"

"No, I... No," said Samson.

"Will you at last tell me the truth?" Delilah demanded.

"I cannot," said Samson. But after a week of constant pleading, sulking and cajoling, Delilah wore him down.

"How can you say you love me when you won't even share your biggest secret?" she demanded, and Samson, at long last, gave in.

"Since the day I was born," he began, "no razor has touched a single hair on my head. If anyone cut my hair, I would surely lose all my strength."

That night, after Samson fell asleep, Delilah summoned the Philistine lords and told them Samson's secret. She held him to her chest while they cut off Samson's beard and flowing locks, then watched as he woke up, seeing his eyes widen in surprise as he realized his strength was gone. Samson was helpless, and he could do nothing to stop the Philistines as they exacted a cruel revenge. They blinded him, then dragged him from his house all the way to their capital city.

For long weeks, Samson was kept in a prison, forced to turn a mill wheel. In his despair, he called out to God. "Why have You deserted me, Lord? Am I not still Your champion?"

God said nothing, but He knew that Samson was not destined to die in a Philistine prison, for his hair had begun to grow back.

Now, the Philistine lords had a plan to mock their greatest enemy in front of thousands. On the day of the feast of Dagon, the god of the Philistines, they brought Samson into their holy temple. They tied him

The Story of Samson

to a pair of pillars in the middle of the temple, while they offered prayers, songs and sacrifices to Dagon.

The people cheered to see their greatest enemy reduced to a blind wreck and began taunting him.

"God give me strength one last time," Samson cried out. "Let me be avenged on these Philistines who stole my eyes. And let me die with them."

The Story of Samson

So saying, he grasped a pillar in each vast hand and pulled with all his might. The pillars came crashing down and the temple collapsed around them all, crushing Samson and his hated enemies in one fell swoop.

David and Goliath

David and Goliath

The Philistine Goliath was an impressive but terrifying sight to behold. He stood head and shoulders above everyone else, and wore a coat of bronze that must have weighed at least as much as two sheep. An enormous spear, with an evil-looking iron point, was clasped in his mighty fist. His legs and arms were covered with bronze too, and the sun glinted off the top of his helmet as he shouted out his challenge to the army of the Israelites.

"Why are you lining up for battle? Choose someone, send him out to me and we will fight, one-on-one. If he kills me, then the Philistines will become your servants. But if I kill him," and something about Goliath's expression said that he was pretty sure that he would, "then *we* shall become *your* masters!"

Despite the fact that Goliath had been shouting out this challenge every morning and evening for the last forty days, the Israelites were terrified. No one dared take the risk of losing, and no one was confident enough to think they might actually win.

"I defy the armies of Israel!" Goliath continued, shaking his fist again. "Give me a man to fight. Let us settle this once and for all!"

And *still* no one stepped forward. In fact, the Israelites broke their battle line and ran back to camp. It was embarrassing. It was humiliating! But worst of all, it meant that the latest war between the Philistines and Israelites was dragging on.

A young man named David had watched the giant's display with growing interest. David's three eldest brothers were soldiers in the Israelite army. Earlier that morning, their father had taken David away from his shepherding duties up in the hills, and told him to take food to the army. But what he really wanted David to do was bring back some reassurance that his sons were all right. So, David had left his sheep behind and heaved a cart laden with bread and cheese down to the Israelites' camp. He had arrived just as the Israelites were about to go off to fight.

"At last," David had thought, "time for some excitement." (Looking after sheep tended to be rather predictable.) Leaving his cart at the camp, he had followed the men to the ridge of the valley and seen them run from Goliath.

Now, back at camp, everyone was gossiping about the challenge, and David couldn't help overhearing.

"Whoever defeats the giant certainly won't regret it," said one.

"Why?" David butted in. "What will happen?"

"Well," another answered, "for one thing, King Saul will give the lucky man his daughter's hand in marriage."

"Really?" David replied, trying not to look too interested. Not only was the king's daughter pretty, whoever married her would also become an extremely powerful man.

"Yes," added a third soldier. "And he won't have to pay any taxes either."

"Nor will his family," piped up a fourth.

"Hmm," thought David. "Now that would make

my father *very* happy..."

"What are *you* doing here?" A harsh voice suddenly interrupted his train of thought. "I know what you're up to, you selfish, lazy boy. How dare you leave the sheep to look after themselves, just so that you can get a glimpse of the battle!" It was Eliab, David's eldest brother.

David sighed. His older brothers could be such a nuisance. "What have I done now?" David said, sullenly. "Am I not allowed to speak?" and he walked away without even bothering to look around, continuing to mingle with the soldiers.

"What will happen to the man who defeats this vile creature who insults Israel?" David asked over and over again. "And who on Earth does this man think he is, to defy God's army?"

David and Goliath

Each time he asked, he heard more or less the same answer. Goliath was a wretched Philistine and his victor, whoever he was, would be richly rewarded.

Meanwhile, a spy for King Saul had been watching David. He reported back to the king everything he heard David say. Saul became intrigued and, soon, David was brought before him.

David seized his opportunity and spoke up at once. "Sire, no one should lose heart just because of this Philistine, Goliath. *I* will fight him!"

David and Goliath

Saul was taken aback by the boy's boldness and wasn't sure what to make of his bravery. "But you are so young," he said, cautiously though not unkindly. "You can't go out and fight Goliath. He's been training to be a soldier since he was a boy."

David had been expecting a reply like this and was ready with his answer. "Your Majesty, I may just be a humble shepherd boy, but I have fought with my life to protect my sheep," he said. "When a lion took off with one of my flock, I attacked it, striking it with my staff so that I could rescue the sheep."

Saul looked suitably impressed.

"And," David continued, "when it turned on me, I grabbed it by its hair and struck it so hard that I killed it!"

"Yes, but..." Saul began.

David and Goliath

"I killed a bear the same way," David interrupted. "And, just as I killed both the lion and the bear, I will kill Goliath! He has defied the army of God, and God, who rescued me from the paws of the lion and the bear, will surely rescue me from the hands of this Philistine!"

"You have to admire David's confidence," Saul thought, shrugging his shoulders. It was a risk – a big risk – but something had to be done to end the stalemate... "Very well, David," he agreed at last. "Off you go! And may the Lord be with you. But at least put on some chain mail first."

To David's surprise, Saul gave him his own tunic and chain mail to wear, but when David fastened on the sword and tried walking around, it felt wrong.

"I can't wear this, Your Majesty," David declared.

David and Goliath

"I'm not used to it. I will fight Goliath in my usual shepherd's tunic. And I will fight him with my sling."

Grasping his shepherd's staff, David bowed to the king and strode from the court.

Near the Israelite camp, he picked five smooth round stones from a stream. Then, with staff in one hand and sling in the other, he approached the giant.

Goliath, meanwhile, had started walking towards David. He snorted in disdain when he saw the young man who dared challenge him. "What? You presume to threaten me

with stones and sticks? What do you think I am?
A dog?" he snarled. "Come here! I'll make minced
meat of you and throw what's left to the animals
and birds."

David, who was desperately hoping that Goliath
couldn't see him tremble, replied with a surprisingly
calm voice. "You threaten me with a sword, a spear
and a javelin. But *I* stand before you in the name of
the Lord Almighty, God of the army of the Israelites
whom you have defied. *I* will defeat *you*! I will strike
you down and cut off your head. And then I will give
the bloody carcasses of the entire Philistine army to
the birds and animals to eat, and the whole world
will know how powerful the God of Israel is. The
battle is His and He will deliver you into our hands."

"That's quite a speech, little man," Goliath

smirked and moved in closer to attack. But before he could get near enough to strike, David reached into his pouch, took out a stone and slung it at Goliath. The stone hit Goliath squarely on the forehead and the giant toppled to his knees, falling face down in the dust. Before he could get up, David had sprinted over, whipped Goliath's sword from its sheath and killed the giant stone dead.

Raising the weighty sword again, he hacked off Goliath's head and held it up in the air by its hair, dripping with blood.

When the Philistines saw what David had done, they turned and fled in terror. But the Israelites surged forward with a deafening roar and chased them all the way back to the city of Gath, where they had come from, slaughtering everyone along the way.

David and Goliath

Then they returned to the Philistine camp and plundered it, taking every scrap of the Philistines' food and all their possessions.

Triumphant, David took Goliath's head to the Israelite city of Jerusalem where, once more, he was brought before the king.

"Whose son are you, boy?" Saul asked, as David knelt before him.

"I am the son of Jesse of Bethlehem," David replied, bowing his head as he held out Goliath's.

"Well, David, son of Jesse, from now on you will be David of Jerusalem and stay by my side," Saul said, smiling.

But in truth, Saul felt uneasy about this all-too likeable and confident young man. Perhaps he had some inkling that one day David would defeat the

Philistines once and for all, and replace Saul as the new king of the Israelites.

Daniel in the Lions' Den

Daniel in the Lions' Den

Long, long ago, King Darius ruled over the great and powerful empire of Persia. To help him rule, he appointed one hundred and twenty officials, known as satraps. And to help him rule his satraps he chose three distinguished men to be administrators and oversee them. One of these men was Daniel.

Daniel was an Israelite, born in the land of Judea, but when he was young, he had been captured and sent to live in Babylon, the capital of Persia. He had been treated well, brought up and educated just like any other Babylonian young gentleman. But, although Daniel was a good and loyal subject, he had stayed true to the customs of his own people. He wouldn't eat Babylonian food, and refused to worship the gods of Babylon, instead remaining faithful to the God of the Israelites.

Daniel was very good at his job. In fact, he was so good, that Darius had plans to promote him and make him the chief administrator. Not surprisingly, this wasn't popular with the other officials. The last thing they wanted was this foreign upstart in charge of them.

"He has to go," they muttered. "There *must* be a way to get rid of him." The problem was, Daniel never seemed to do anything wrong. He was well-known for being trustworthy, he was famous for always being extra careful to carry out his duties properly, and he never ever seemed to make mistakes. It was infuriating. Whatever the satraps tried, in the hope of distracting him, nothing worked.

One day, all the satraps got together to discuss how they could be rid of this tiresome man. "It's hopeless," they moaned. "We're never going to make him look bad."

Then one satrap, who had been standing at the back of the group, began to weave his way to the front. "Unless!" he said, in a loud voice to get their attention. "Unless..." he went on more quietly, to be sure they were all listening carefully. "Unless we force him to choose between his religion and his loyalty to the king."

With all eyes now on him, he continued, "You all know that Daniel is loyal to our king and country, but there is one thing he will never do. He will never go against the laws of his religion." The others murmured and nodded their agreement. It was true, but how could it help them to get rid of Daniel?

The satrap smiled. "Here's what we have to do…" he said. The others moved in closer to hear his idea.

Now, Daniel was in the habit of praying to God every day without fail. Three times a day, come wind, rain or sandstorm, he would go home. There, in an upstairs room, he would throw open his windows and kneel down on his prayer mat. Then, facing his old home city, Jerusalem, he would pray. It was no secret – although Daniel, being a pious man, made no show of it.

This, the satrap explained, would be Daniel's downfall.

"But how?" the others asked. "He's not doing anything he's not allowed to do!"

"No," said the satrap. "Not yet..."

The next day, the satraps all met up outside Darius' throne room and, in a nervous huddle, were ushered through to speak to him.

"Yes?" Darius asked imperiously.

One of the satraps shuffled forwards. "M... m... may King Darius live forever!" he quivered.

Darius sighed, looking bored.

Another satrap pushed the first one aside. "Darius,

oh lord and king of Persia, we, that is to say, your faithful servants, your satraps and I, believe that in recognition of your supreme deity, it should be announced that for the next thirty days, no one should pray to any god or human but you."

Darius looked surprised, but also rather pleased.

"And," the satrap continued, "if I may boldly suggest, you should make this law."

Darius remained silent as he considered this unusual proposal.

"And, furthermore, that anyone who breaks your law should be thrown into the lions' den."

Darius threw back his head and laughed. "Why not?" he said. "After all, it's no more than I deserve, and it's about time I flushed out those who are not loyal to me."

The satrap suppressed a smile. That had been easier than he thought. "Well then, Your Majesty, perhaps you could sign this." He produced a document with a flourish and wafted it under the king's nose. "Just so that the law becomes official…"

Darius signed the document.

"…and cannot be taken back," the satrap added.

When Daniel heard of the new law, he shrugged his shoulders. After all, there was nothing he could do about it. He continued to pray to God in his upstairs room as usual – which was exactly what the satraps wanted. As soon as they'd seen him, they hurried back to the king.

"Oh majestic sovereign of the land of the greatest wonders of the world, we regret to inform you that your servant Daniel has disobeyed you and broken

your law," they told him. "This exiled Judean continues to pray to his foreign God every day, just as if nothing has changed," they added, pretending to look shocked and outraged.

Now, Darius really didn't want anything bad to happen to Daniel, but the law was the law, and there was nothing he could do to change it. Not even the king of Persia could do that, if he wanted to remain king. So, reluctantly, he gave the order, and Daniel was dragged from his room, down the stairs and out of his house.

As the guards threw Daniel into the lions' den, Darius solemnly called out, "May your God, whom you serve continually, rescue you!" He truly wished that he would, but he didn't hold out much hope.

A huge stone was dragged across the entrance to the pit, and the king sealed it with his own ring, to make sure there was no way that Daniel could escape or be rescued.

Darius returned home with a heavy heart. He spent the night alone, after dismissing all the singers and dancers that usually kept him entertained, and even refused to eat. He went to bed early, but tossed and turned all night. As soon the sun started to rise, he got up and hurried back to the lions' den.

Anxiously, he cried, "Daniel, my servant, has your God, whom you serve continually, been able to rescue you from the lions?"

He wasn't expecting a reply. Horrible visions of Daniel being ripped apart by the lions' fearsome jaws had plagued him all night. But, to his astonishment, he heard a muffled voice call out, "May King Darius live forever! God sent His angel, and He shut the mouths of the lions. They have not hurt me, because I was found innocent in His sight. Nor have I ever done any wrong before you, Your Majesty."

Daniel was alive!

"Quick! Quick! Get that rock out of the way," Darius ordered, staring down into the den and looking at Daniel in amazement. Not only was he alive and well, but there wasn't a single scratch or

Daniel in the Lions' Den

tooth mark on him – just a few stray lion hairs, where the lions had nuzzled and rubbed against his robe.

"This is truly a miracle," Darius shouted, overjoyed, as Daniel was pulled from the den. "Daniel's God must be a great god. In fact, from now on, let all the people of Persia worship and fear Daniel's God. Let everyone in the world respect Him! For *He* is the living God!"

Meanwhile, the satraps had been rounded up and arrested. They were thrown into the lions' den along with their families. The screams were terrible – the lions were hungry after spending the entire night without food.

And as for Daniel... He lived in comfort and safety throughout the rest of King Darius' reign.

Jonah and the Whale

Jonah and the Whale

"I want you to go to Nineveh," God ordered his prophet Jonah. "Go and tell the people in that wicked place to repent of all their sins. If they do not, I shall destroy it."

"No!" Jonah refused, heading as fast as he could in the opposite direction. In no time at all, Jonah had boarded a merchant ship loaded up with goods bound for a distant land, intending to get as far away from Nineveh as he could.

He huddled up in a corner, deep in the ship's hold, muttering to himself. "Why doesn't God leave me alone? I'm an old man, and I'm tired. I've already worked hard all my life, preaching to everyone in Jerusalem, and now He expects me to go all the way to Nineveh. Besides, He won't really harm it." Eventually, the rolling of the waves sent Jonah into a deep sleep.

Up on deck, the captain was growing anxious. A tremendous storm had blown up, and strong winds tore across the bows. The waves started to rise higher and higher, water slopping dangerously over the edge.

Each crewman began to pray loudly to his own god – as many gods in all as the countries the sailors had been born in. But no one answered their prayers. Instead, the wind howled ever louder, and the waves grew ever larger.

"Why is this happening to us?" the captain called out. "Who on board has made the gods so angry?"

Then he remembered the stranger in the hold.

Two sailors found Jonah fast asleep, and dragged him onto the storm-ravaged deck. "Wake up, old man!" the captain shouted. "I know it's you who has brought this terrible wind down on us. Tell us who you are, and what you have done to make the gods punish us."

"Not *gods*, but the one true God," said Jonah. "I am an Israelite, and I tell you it is *my* God who has raised this storm... I disobeyed Him. He asked me to go one way, but I wanted to go the other, and now He's punishing us all. Throw me into the sea," Jonah finished. "If you do, God is sure to calm the storm, and you will all be safe."

"I won't commit murder," said the captain. He left Jonah sitting on the deck, crying, while he barked out orders. The crew set to work, heaving crates of cargo into the waves, hoping to lighten the ship. Then each man grabbed an oar and began to row, in a last, desperate, attempt to pull the boat out of the storm.

But nothing worked. The captain knew that just one big wave would be enough to capsize his ship, and it would come sooner rather than later.

"Forgive me, old man," he said through gritted teeth. "I have no choice left."

Jonah and the Whale

And he hoisted Jonah onto his shoulders and flung him overboard.

The captain began to pray, begging forgiveness for sending Jonah to his death. He watched the aged prophet swirl this way and that in the churning waves below. And then, just as Jonah started slipping beneath the surface, the sea became calmer.

The prophet, sure he was about to die, closed his eyes and let the raging sea surround his body.

Jonah and the Whale

He felt himself rise and fall with the waves, sensed a tangle of weeds wrapping themselves around his body, then a warmth as he was sucked deeper underwater.

"This is it," thought Jonah. "I'm going to meet my Maker, and He won't be pleased with me..."

But Jonah was wrong. God had decided to give him a second chance. He sent an enormous whale to rescue the reluctant prophet. When Jonah thought he was being wrapped in weeds and sucked into the depths, he was actually being swallowed by the whale.

For three days and nights, Jonah sat in the belly of the whale, wondering why he wasn't dead, but also stubbornly refusing to talk to God. On the third night, Jonah realized that God was not going to let him escape from this underwater prison. At last, he

Jonah and the Whale

decided to pray.

"God, You have saved my life. I should never have tried to run away from You. I will do what You told me to. I will go to Nineveh." The next morning, the whale swam to shore and spat Jonah up onto a sandy beach.

Nineveh turned out to be an enormous city.

Jonah spent a whole day walking up and down the streets. "In forty days, God will bring down this city of evil!" he preached. "Stop being greedy, stop being selfish, and the Lord will save you."

Jonah was used to being ignored by the people he preached to. So he was taken entirely by surprise when, on just his second day in town, the king of Nineveh listened.

"Hear me, people of Nineveh," proclaimed the

king. "Jonah is right! We *have* been greedy and selfish. We must do as he says."

The king threw down his golden crown, and ripped off his fine clothes. For the next month, he dressed himself in an old sackcloth. Instead of his magnificent throne, he sat on a pile of ashes. He refused to eat or drink anything at all, and ordered everyone in the city to do the same.

God watched everything, and was pleased. "Jonah, tell the people of Nineveh that I have heard their prayers, and have seen that they are truly sorry. I will spare this town. You can go home now."

"What?!" Jonah shrieked. "You mean to say, You sent me here, You made me sit inside that stinking whale for three days, and all for *nothing*? I know You are a merciful God, and I always knew You were never really going to destroy Nineveh. That's why I ran away in the first place!"

"Why are you so angry, Jonah?" God asked.

But Jonah ignored God. He sat in the desert outside Nineveh, sulking. By the middle of the day, Jonah was starting to faint in the heat of the sun.

God made a plant grow next to Jonah. A large leaf sprouted above his head, shading him, and Jonah sighed with relief. But when night fell,

and Jonah had fallen asleep, God sent a worm to eat the plant. The next day, Jonah sat in the sun again, and this time the heat made him so hot and thirsty that he cried out in agony.

"Why did that poor little plant have to die?" he wailed. "Life is so unfair! I wish I was dead!"

"Jonah, you should learn not to be so angry all the time," said God. "Think how sad you are just because a plant died. Now, think about all the hundreds of thousands of people who live in Nineveh. Would you have been happy if they all died? And because of your preaching, they repented and were saved. Now, go home and rest. You've earned it."

Map of the Old Testament Lands

Syria

Damascus •

Mediterranean Sea

Canaan

River Jordan

Jericho •
Jerusalem • ▲ Mount Moriah
• Gath • Bethlehem
• Gaza
Judea
• Sodom
• Gomorrah

Philistia

Dead Sea

Etham •

The Dead Sea is thought to have expanded after the destruction of Sodom and Gomorrah.

Egypt

Midian Desert

• Rephidim
▲ Mount Sinai
(also called
Mount Horeb)

Red Sea

Assyria

• Nineveh

River Tigris

River Euphrates

Some scholars believe
the Garden of Eden was
located between these
two rivers.

Persia

Babylon •

Babylon is a
possible site of
the Tower of
Babel.

Babylonia

Arabian Desert

Who's Who in the Old Testament

 Aaron: brother of Moses, and spokesman for the Israelites

Abraham: originally known as Abram; a faithful servant to God

 Adam: the first man, made by God to live in Eden with Eve

Benjamin: younger brother of Joseph, and the youngest of the twelve sons of Jacob

 Daniel: an Israelite working in Babylon some years after Judea was conquered by the Persians

Darius: king of Persia, and ruler of all the lands from Egypt to India

David: a shepherd boy who defeated Goliath and became the second king of the Israelites, conquering the Philistines

 Delilah: the second wife of Samson the Israelite, she betrayed her husband for money

Eliezer: younger son of Moses and Zipporah

Eve: the first woman, made by God to live in Eden with Adam

Gershom: elder son of Moses and Zipporah

 Goliath: a huge and powerful warrior, champion of the Philistine army

Isaac: son of Abraham, father of Jacob and grandfather of Joseph

Israelites: all the descendants of Jacob

Jacob: son of Isaac, later given a new name by God: Israel

Jethro: Moses' father-in-law

Jonah: one of God's prophets, swallowed by a whale

Joseph: son of Jacob, and one of twelve brothers, including Reuben, Judah, Simeon and Benjamin

Joshua: leader of the Israelites after Moses died

Lot: nephew of Abraham, and the only man to escape from Sodom and Gomorrah

Miriam: sister of Moses, who tricked the Pharaoh's daughter into bringing up baby Moses as her son

Moses: a descendant of Jacob; raised the son of the Pharaoh, he became an Israelite leader

Noah: a loyal servant of God, who built an ark to survive the great flood

Pharaoh: the word for the king of Egypt

Philistines: long-time enemies of the Israelites

Potiphar: a high-ranking Egyptian soldier who bought Joseph to be his slave

Rahab: a woman who lived in Jericho but agreed to work as a spy for Joshua and the Israelites

Reuben: the eldest son of Jacob, he sold his half-brother Joseph into slavery

Samson: an incredibly strong Israelite, who fought and killed many Philistines

Sarah: wife of Abraham, and mother of Isaac

Saul: first king of the Israelites

Zipporah: wife of Moses

The New Testament

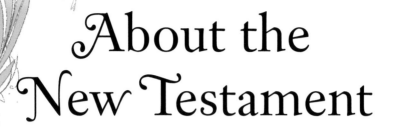

About the New Testament

When the New Testament opens, hundreds of years have passed. The Israelites have lost much of their once glorious kingdom. Now they are huddled together in two small provinces named Judea and Galilee, and known by their oppressors as the Jews.

God is still watching over them all. He decides to show His love for His creation by becoming part of it, sending His son, Jesus Christ, to live on Earth.

Jesus performs miracles and tells stories to the thousands of people he meets, to try to teach them about God and himself.

After his death, four men, named Matthew, Mark, Luke and John, collect as many stories about Jesus as they can. Their collections, known as the Gospels, open the New Testament.

They sometimes tell slightly different versions of events, but one thing stays the same – Jesus is a powerful, inspirational and loving man.

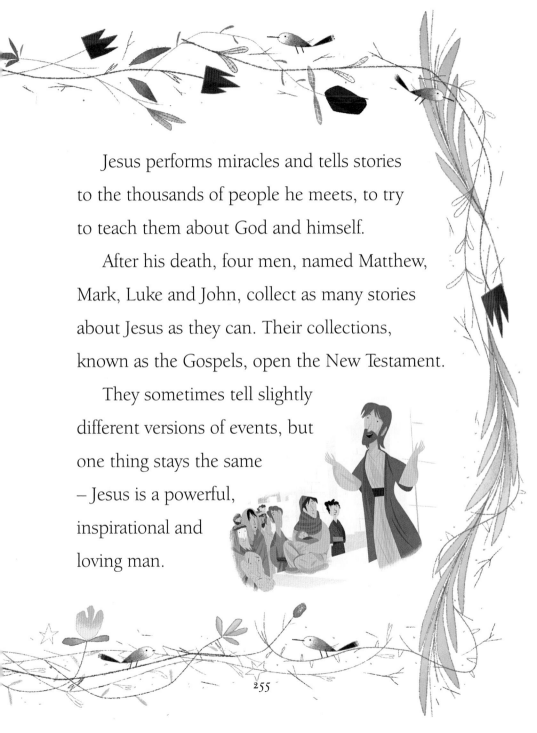

The Birth of Jesus

The Birth of Jesus

The Jews of Judea were praying for someone to save them. They desperately needed a strong, fearless leader who could free their land from the cruel ruler, King Herod, and from the Romans, people of a mighty empire who had conquered them some years ago. But where would they find such a hero?

Even the Jewish priests, who had studied all the sayings of the ancient prophets, did not know the exact answer. Most thought this hero would be a king – a direct descendant of David, the greatest of all the kings of the Israelites.

The Birth of Jesus

King David had been born in the town of Bethlehem – perhaps their new leader would be born there, too? But a thousand years had passed since those days and David's descendants had scattered far and wide.

One of them, a lowly carpenter named Joseph, lived in a small town in the north, named Nazareth. Joseph was too excited to worry about Romans, kings or heroes. He had just received the most wonderful news – the girl he loved, Mary, had agreed to marry him. Joseph was looking forward to setting up a house with his new bride, and dreamed about the children they might have together one day.

Meanwhile, Mary was awash with emotions. There was joy, at the thought of marrying Joseph, the kindest man she knew. There was excitement at the prospect of leaving her home – but sadness, too, at leaving her parents behind. And there was a hint of fear about the future, and what her life might have in store.

One day, with all these thoughts swirling through her head, Mary went out for a walk, hoping to find some time and space alone to think. Just as she was starting to feel calm, a figure, dressed in blazing white, appeared and hovered before her.

"Greetings, Mary," the figure called out. "The Lord your God is here. Blessed are you amongst women!"

Mary fell to her knees and hid her face in her hands. She didn't know what to make of this stranger and his peculiar words.

The Birth of Jesus

"Don't be afraid, Mary," said the figure. "I am Gabriel, God's angel. He loves you very dearly, and He has sent me to bring you joyful news! You are going to have a baby – a son – and his name will be Jesus. He will be a great king. His kingdom will have no borders, and his reign will last for all time."

"I don't understand," said Mary. "I can't have a baby. It's not possible! I'm not married yet."

"Nothing is impossible for God, Mary," proclaimed the angel. "You see, your baby will be God's own child."

Mary gasped.

"God has already made the impossible happen," Gabriel continued. "Go to visit your cousin Elizabeth. She is an old woman now, and every doctor declared that she could never have a child – but God has promised her she will! Go and see for yourself."

The Birth of Jesus

Mary bowed her head, trembling. Then she said, humbly, "I am God's servant, and I will accept whatever fate He has in store for me."

On hearing these words, Gabriel vanished, and Mary was alone again, more confused than ever. She stumbled, crying, back to Nazareth.

In no time at all she was wrapped up in Joseph's arms, sobbing. "Joseph, Joseph, dear Joseph," she choked out. "Something strange and wonderful has happened... I can't find the words to explain it."

Joseph wiped tears away from her eyes, trying to decide if she was happy or sad. "What *is* it?" he asked.

Mary spoke breathlessly, still crying yet smiling at the same time. "I am going to have a baby! I have to go and see my cousin, Elizabeth, now. She's having a baby, too. Isn't it incredible?"

The Birth of Jesus

"What? But…" Joseph was speechless. He knew that Mary would not tell a lie, but he couldn't quite believe what he was hearing. He stood in silence as Mary kissed his cheek and hurried away to her cousin's house.

That night, Joseph lay awake in his bed, still wondering what was happening. "What about the wedding?" he thought. "Can I marry a woman who is having someone else's child?" With these questions racing through his mind, Joseph sank into a dream-filled sleep.

In his dreams, he heard a voice calling to him. "Joseph, son of David, listen to me. I am God's messenger, and I tell you, *do not be afraid to marry your beloved Mary*. She *is* going to have a child – but the child will be the Son of God. He will save the world from all evil."

The Birth of Jesus

Joseph sat bolt upright in his bed, his mind clear. He knew that this was not just a dream – an angel really had spoken to him, and had told him the truth, however crazy it sounded.

The next morning, he made his way to Elizabeth's house in the hills outside Nazareth, and knocked on the door. "Mary, Mary!" he cried. "Let me in."

Mary opened the door, and Joseph hugged her tightly. Behind her, Joseph could see Elizabeth, her belly swollen with the child that would soon be born.

"A double miracle," said Joseph, smiling. "Now, let's get married!"

And so, one wedding and eight months later, Joseph and Mary were

preparing for their son to be born.

Meanwhile, life in Israel was getting harder. The Roman Emperor, Augustus, had demanded that every family pay him a new tax. To make sure that everyone was accounted for, Roman soldiers were riding up and down the land, telling all the men to go to the town of their ancestors, taking their wives and children with them.

Joseph had to travel all the way to Bethlehem, the home of his distant ancestor, King David. With Mary riding on a donkey, and the baby due at any moment, they set off on the five-day journey to the south.

The Birth of Jesus

They finally arrived very late one night, only to find the town was full – of Joseph's long-lost cousins. They called in at every inn they saw, but there was no room for them anywhere.

At last, shortly before midnight, an innkeeper on the edge of town took pity on them. "It's not much to offer," he said, "but you could stay in the stable behind my inn. There's straw on the ground and at least it would be a roof over your heads."

Mary gave birth just a few hours later. She wrapped the baby in a clean white cloth, and put him into the animals' manger to sleep, nestled on a bed of hay. Exhausted, Mary collapsed onto the straw piled up beside the manger.

Gabriel, God's angel, had been keeping a careful eye on Mary and Joseph. He wanted to spread the happy news immediately, and flew to the fields

outside Bethlehem where some shepherds were
still awake, watching their flocks.

A blinding light filled the night sky, and the
shepherds cried out in fear, too scared even to
run away.

"Don't be afraid!" Gabriel called to them. "This is
a time for rejoicing! I have the most wonderful news
to share. At last, the leader that the Israelites have
been waiting for, all these long years, has been born!

He was born this very night, in the city of David.

The Birth of Jesus

Go into town and you will find him.
He is wrapped in white cloths, and
lies asleep in a manger."

With these words, the sky lit up even
more brightly, as Gabriel was joined by a choir
of angels, all singing songs of praise.

"Glory to God in Heaven," they sang. "Peace on
Earth, and good will to all the peoples of the world!"

The shepherds were overwhelmed by the

spectacle, and their hearts were filled with wonder.

"Can it be true?" asked one.

"Surely such a child won't be lying in a stable –
he ought to be in a palace!" scoffed another.

"Let's go and see for ourselves," said a third,
racing the others into Bethlehem. And there, in a
stable behind an inn, they saw a mother sitting on the
hay next to a newborn baby in a manger, just as the
angel had described.

"It's true," they cried. "It's really true!" They
ran all around the town, shouting to anyone they
bumped into that a child had been born who would
save the world. They were so amazed by what they
had seen, that they went on to the next town, and the
next, telling everyone that a new king had been born
in Bethlehem.

Very quickly, their story reached the ears of King

The Birth of Jesus

Herod himself. He didn't really believe the ravings of these wandering shepherds, but doubt niggled at him. The doubt grew into serious concern on the day that three magnificent strangers arrived at his palace.

They rode camels, and were dressed in beautiful robes embroidered with strange patterns. "They look like kings from distant lands," thought Herod. "What are they doing here?" He listened very carefully to what they had to say.

"Where is the child that has been born to be the king of the Jews?" asked the first man.

"We have come to worship him," said the second, solemnly.

"I haven't heard anything about a new king," lied Herod. "Where did you hear this story?"

"Some days ago, we saw a new star in the night sky," explained the third man. "We have studied the

heavens for many years and we believe this star is a
sign of a great king. So, we followed it here, to Israel."

"Please," asked the first man, "can you tell us
where this king has been born?"

Herod turned to his chief priests. "Well, you've
heard what these learned men think. What do you
have to say?" he demanded.

"The scriptures say a king will be born in David's
city, Bethlehem," one declared.

Herod shrugged. "Try the town of
Bethlehem," he told the three
men. "If the child really
exists, you will find him
there. And if you do
find him, please come

back this way and tell me, so that I may worship him, too."

The three men left Herod's palace and started on the road to Bethlehem. That evening, as the stars began to twinkle in the heavens, the new star appeared again. They followed it, as it moved across the midnight sky, until it came to rest above the place where Mary, Joseph and Jesus were staying.

The Birth of Jesus

The men climbed from their camels and went inside, kneeling on the floor.

"Hail to the king!" they proclaimed in unison, bowing low.

"Oh, please, stand up," said Joseph. "We are not nobles that you have to kneel before."

But the three wise men remained on their knees. "Maybe you don't realize," the first man spoke up, "but this child is destined to be the noblest man who ever lived."

"Won't you tell us who you are?" asked Mary.

"Caspar," said the first, "of India."

"Melchior," said the second, "of Persia."

"Balthazar," said the third, "of Arabia."

"Will you accept a few gifts for your son?" Caspar went on. "I have brought a casket of gold, fit for a king..."

The Birth of Jesus

"And this is frankincense," added Melchior, "a delightful scent fit for God in Heaven..."

"And my offering is myrrh, a fragrant resin for the child who will live and die to save us all," said Balthazar.

Mary and Joseph couldn't believe their eyes. They had never seen such fine and precious things in all their lives. It was only now that Mary began to understand the words Gabriel had told her those long months ago – her son, Jesus, would be a king bringing hope to people everywhere, all across the Earth.

That night, Gabriel visited Mary and Joseph one last time.

The Birth of Jesus

"King Herod is looking for Jesus," he warned them. "He feels threatened. You cannot go home yet. Head to Egypt, far from Herod's grasp, and keep the child safe."

Caspar, Melchior and Balthazar had already left Bethlehem, but they didn't return to King Herod as he had asked.

"I don't trust him," said one of the wise men, and the others agreed. It was obvious that Herod guarded his power jealously. He would not welcome a rival.

When Herod found out that the men from the East had gone, he was furious. He sent his soldiers into Bethlehem to seize all the baby boys born in recent months, believing that one of them must be the promised king.

Herod didn't know it, but baby Jesus and his parents were already on the road to Egypt. In a fit of rage, the cruel king ordered his soldiers to kill all the boys they had seized. But it wasn't enough – Herod lived the rest of his days in constant fear that the true king would come and take his throne.

Only a few months later, the news reached Mary

and Joseph that King Herod was dead. At last, the young family made their way home to Nazareth. Baby Jesus could grow up in peace.

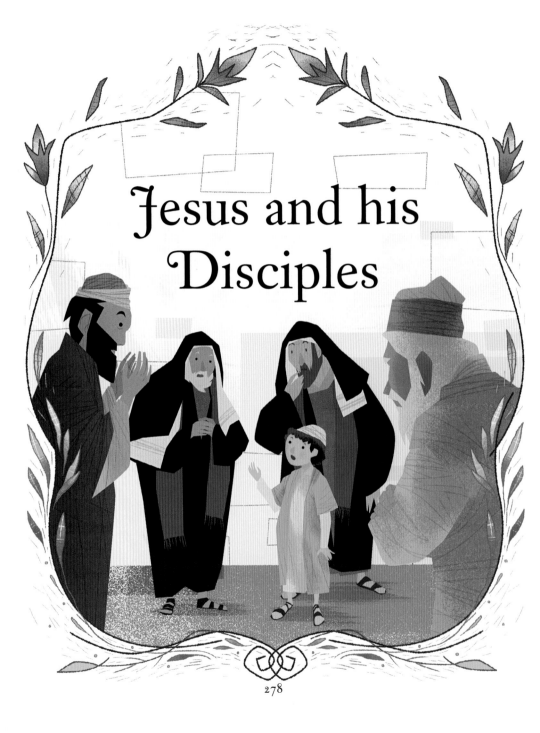

Jesus and his Disciples

Jesus and his Disciples

As Jesus grew older, his parents began to forget the angel's promise that their child was the Son of God. Jesus himself tried not to think about it. Instead, he spent his time meeting people and hearing their stories. Everyone found him easy to talk to. But one day Jesus was so busy being friendly that he got into trouble.

He was about twelve years old, and had gone to Jerusalem with his parents to celebrate the annual festival of Passover. A large crowd of friends and family made the journey together.

On the way home, Mary grew worried. "Joseph, have you seen Jesus?" she asked, panic in her voice. "I haven't seen him since we left Jerusalem."

"Oh, he'll be with his friends," Joseph reassured her. But he started to ask around, and grew equally worried when no one knew where Jesus was.

Frantically, they retraced their steps and found Jesus exactly where they had last seen him – talking to priests in the temple. He had been there for two whole days, completely unaware his family had left.

"Your son is a marvel," one of the priests said. "He asks perceptive questions, and gives the most intelligent answers to the questions we ask him."

By the time Jesus had grown up, it was clear to Mary that he had no interest in becoming a carpenter like his father, or even in having a normal job at all.

If anything, he took after his cousin, John.

John had set himself up near the River Jordan as a prophet. He prayed to God day and night, and told people what God said to him.

"You are all sinners!" John would wail to anyone who passed. "But God will forgive you if you are sorry and wash yourselves clean. Now is the time to live righteously, because God is coming."

The chief priests in Jerusalem didn't like John, but they were impressed at the crowds he drew – crowds of people who genuinely wanted to get closer to God. So the chief priests sent along a team of junior priests, known as Pharisees, to see what John did.

Almost immediately, they were confronted with a bizarre spectacle. A long line of men and women waded into the middle of the River Jordan, where

John was standing. One by one, he poured water over their heads, saying, "I baptize you. Repent and be born again into God's loving arms!"

The Pharisees had heard people talk about 'John the Baptist', but until they saw him perform a baptism, they didn't know what it meant.

"Who are you to welcome people into God's arms?" demanded the Pharisees. "Are you the hero that was promised to the prophets of old?"

"I am no hero," said John, firmly. "I'm simply a man, doing my best to tell as many people as I can that they need to get ready."

"For what?" asked the Pharisees, confused.

"For the hero you speak of. He has already been born! Even now, he is out there, somewhere, and he will change the world. Compared to him, the work I'm doing is nothing."

The very next day, Jesus himself was in the crowd beside the Jordan. John blinked in astonishment when he saw Jesus wading out to him.

"Jesus, I can't baptize you!" John protested. "God has told me about you. If anything, *you* should be the one to baptize *me*!"

"Please," said Jesus.

"God has given you the gift of baptism, so you should baptize anyone who asks."

John agreed, and washed Jesus in the river. As Jesus walked out onto the bank, John saw him glowing in the sunlight. He looked up into the sky and saw a vision of God Himself sending His spirit down onto Jesus. It looked like a dove.

Not long after that, the Pharisees returned and flung John into prison. So many people had gone to be baptized that the chief priests in Jerusalem felt threatened, and had decided to silence him.

Jesus, meanwhile, had gone to start a new life near the Sea of Galilee. He went there with Andrew, a friend he had made while listening to John.

Andrew told Jesus about the mountains that flanked the eastern shore of the sea, and about his family, who lived in a fishing village on the west bank.

Andrew introduced Jesus to his brother, Simon. and Jesus smiled, as if meeting an old friend.

"Hello, Simon," he said. "I can already tell you will be a solid friend, a true rock. I'm going to call you Peter – the rock!"

Peter, a simple but loving man, was instantly taken with Jesus. "Call me what you like," he said, smiling through a bushy beard. "I don't know why, but I believe I'd follow you just about anywhere."

The three friends walked along the shore where a man named Zebedee had just put out to sea with his sons, James and John.

"Drop your nets and come with me," Jesus called. "If you stay on your boat, you will catch fish, enough to feed your village. But if you join me, I will help you

find something that can feed the whole world."

Zebedee ignored Jesus and went on fussing with the nets. But James and John were intrigued. They leaped out of the boat and swam over to Jesus.

Now with four followers, Jesus headed to the nearest town, Bethsaida. Andrew called on his friend, Philip, who rushed to find *his* friend, Nathaniel.

"Come with me, Nathaniel," said Philip, excitedly. "You have to meet this man Jesus, from Nazareth."

"Nazareth?" laughed Nathaniel. "No one important has ever come from Nazareth!" But he agreed to go with Philip, out of curiosity.

Jesus and his Disciples

"Look," Jesus said to Andrew, as Nathaniel approached. "Here comes an Israelite worthy of the name, an honest man who looks out for his friends."

Flattered and surprised, Nathaniel asked, "How can you possibly know anything about me?"

Jesus laughed. "It's no trick. I noticed you this morning over by that fig tree. I saw the way you were with people, and could tell you are a good man."

"You really are something special," said Nathaniel.

"You think that's special?" said Jesus. "Follow me, and I will show you greater wonders than this!"

Over the next few weeks, Jesus found six more men who became his closest companions. They called themselves the twelve disciples, and together they truly believed that they would change the world.

A Wedding in Cana

A Wedding in Cana

In the town of Cana, in Galilee, two young people were getting ready for their wedding. In fact, the whole town was getting ready. A newly married couple always provided a generous feast for their guests and everyone was helping with the preparations. Five fat sheep were chosen to be cooked with garlic and spices, long loaves were lined up, ready for baking, and twenty jugs of the best red wine were safely stashed away.

Among the joyful guests were Jesus, his mother, Mary, and all twelve disciples.

A Wedding in Cana

Once the marriage ceremony was over, the feasting and dancing could begin. The master of the feast, a large man with a loud voice, bustled around, making sure everyone had plenty to eat and drink.

Jesus sat with his disciples, watching the party. The men lifted the bride and groom on chairs and danced with them high in the air. The bride laughed and shrieked as they spun her around.

"Bring out more wine!" cried the master of the feast, after a few hours of dancing.

One of the servants went to the storeroom, but Mary noticed him return moments later, looking pale. He spoke with the other servants, and they glanced nervously at the empty wine cups scattered across the long tables. Mary went over to see what was wrong.

"The wine has run out," she said, hurrying back to

the disciples. It was a disaster to run out of food or wine at a wedding party – and very embarrassing for the bride and groom and their families.

"Jesus, can't you do something?" Mary asked.

Despite himself, Jesus was annoyed. "What does it have to do with me if the wine has run out?" he muttered under his breath.

He knew what Mary was really saying. She wanted him to do something miraculous to save the wedding party and Jesus wasn't sure he felt ready to show everyone that he was different.

But Mary trusted that Jesus would respond to her plea for help. "Do whatever he tells you," she told the servants.

Jesus sighed and followed them to the storeroom. It was true: every last drop of wine had been drunk.

Six large stone jars stood against one wall. "Fill them up with water," Jesus said.

The servants weren't convinced. The guests wouldn't be very happy drinking only water... but they did as Jesus asked. Soon, the jars were filled to the brim.

"Now take a cup and draw some out," said Jesus.

A servant bent down and removed the cork at the bottom of one of the jars. As the liquid poured out and sploshed into his cup, it changed from clear pure water to a deep swirling red. The water had turned into wine.

The servants were astounded. They rushed to the other water jars and peered inside. Each one was filled to the top with wine!

Jesus didn't seem to notice everyone's amazement.

A Wedding in Cana

"Take this wine to the master of the feast," he told the servants.

Back at the party, the master of the feast took a big gulp of wine. His eyes grew wide with pleasure. "That is delicious," he boomed, smacking his lips. "Sir!" he yelled over the din, beckoning to the groom who was caught in the middle of the dancing.

"You generous fellow! Most people serve the good wine first and then the bad wine later, when people are too tired to notice, but you have saved the best until last."

The groom, who was being whisked away by the crowd of dancing bodies, couldn't really hear what the man was saying, so he simply smiled and nodded.

The disciples shook their heads in disbelief. All the wine had run out, yet here were six jars overflowing with wine!

The party continued until morning. The bride and groom's faces shone with delight when their guests said it was one of the finest wedding parties they had ever attended.

Jesus left the noisy celebrations and sat watching the sun rise. He thought hard about the miracle he had performed, his very first. This time, it was only the servants who had seen what had happened, but soon, more and more people would know about the miracle of God.

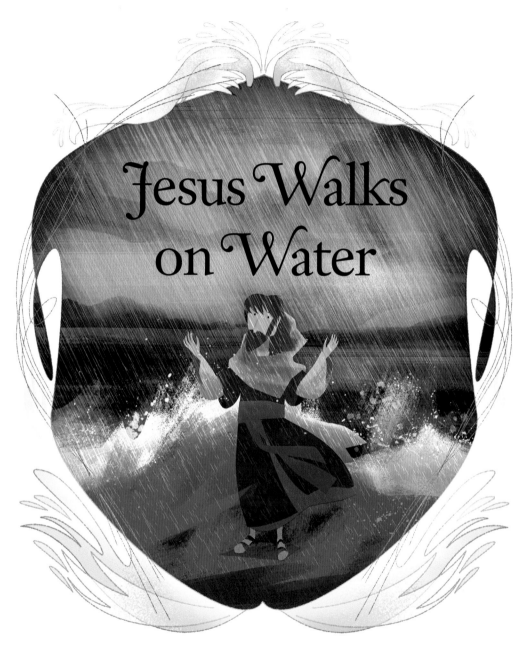

Jesus Walks on Water

On the sandy shores of the Sea of Galilee, Peter, one of Jesus' disciples, was feeling uneasy. "Are you sure you won't change your mind?" he asked, staring out across the water.

Jesus shook his head. "No, Peter. I have already told you, I will not be joining you on this journey. I must speak to God, alone."

"But..." Peter started, then stopped, knowing better than to argue with Jesus.

Jesus smiled at his dear disciple. "Come now, Peter, no harm will befall you. Any of you..." he said, indicating the rest of the disciples, already boarding the boat that would take them across the sea. "It is your task to travel on, taking the word of God with you. Trust that He will protect you."

His faith strengthened by Jesus' words, Peter joined his friends. They rowed away from the shore, waving farewell to their teacher.

With his disciples sent on their way, Jesus set off on his own journey. He scaled a nearby mountain and knelt down to pray. It was only when he heard a distant rumble of thunder that he opened his eyes.

He glanced up at the darkening sky and saw, over the sea, a menacing storm cloud. At once he feared for his disciples.

Meanwhile, out in the middle of the Sea of Galilee,

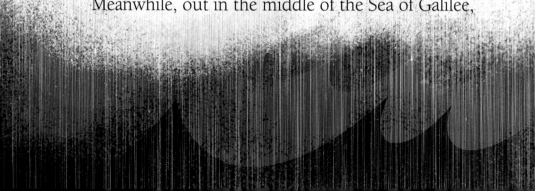

the boat was struggling against the wind-whipped waves of a full-blown storm. Some disciples were huddled together, petrified by the booming thunder and blinding lightning. Others were bailing water out of the boat, trying desperately to keep it afloat.

Peter held tightly to his oar. "Together we can beat this storm," he promised. "Take an oar and row with me and we will reach the other side unharmed!"

But none of the disciples responded, for his words were drowned out by the savagery of the storm.

"Please Lord, help us," prayed Peter, his eyes clenched tightly shut against the spray of the waves. He repeated his prayer again and again, until a great

shout of terror cut through the roar of the wind.

"What is it?" he called. The disciples were staring out into the storm, their mouths open in shock.

Peter followed their gaze across the sea to where a pillar of light shone brightly on the water. "Is it some strange lightning?" he thought. "Or a ghost? A spirit?"

Whatever it was, it was moving closer. The longer Peter stared, the larger it seemed to loom, until finally it started to resemble... "Jesus?"

"Jesus?" echoed the disciples. "It's not possible," they chorused. "The storm isn't even touching him!"

"Forget that," shouted Peter. "He's not in a boat!"

The disciples gasped in unison. It was true. Jesus was walking across the water's surface as though it were a paved street.

"Do not be fooled," one disciple cried. "That's not

Jesus, but some foul spirit. It's death, come to us on foot." His fear spread through the boat like a plague.

Suddenly, a voice cut through the storm. "Be of good cheer," it called. "It is I. Do not be afraid."

The disciples fell silent, except for Peter, who raised his voice in reply. "If you are Jesus, then prove it to us. Have me join you on the water."

For a time, the only sounds came from the sky and sea. Then, at last: "Come. Put your faith in me."

Peter looked over the side of the boat at the tall, cresting waves. Then he looked back to the shining spirit. Bracing himself, he stepped over the edge...

And he kept walking, unafraid and unharmed by the wind or the water, until he was by the spirit's side. Then he knew, without a doubt, it was truly Jesus.

But at that same moment he remembered the

Jesus Walks on Water

blustering storm and saw how far he was from the boat. His fears resurfaced and at once he felt the cold bite of water around his ankles – he was sinking!

With a splash and a yelp, Peter slipped beneath the wild waves. "Jesus!" he cried. "Lord, save me!"

Jesus reached down and plucked Peter from the water as easily as a man plucks fruit from a tree. "So little faith," he said, with a smile and a shake of his head. "Didn't I say that God would protect you?"

Peter held tightly to Jesus as the two returned to the boat. As Jesus stepped on board, the wind dropped, the clouds parted, and the storm faded away as though it had never been.

The disciples cheered. "I should never have doubted it," said one. "You really are the Son of God."

Loaves and Fish

Loaves and Fish

Jesus had just heard some very sad news. His cousin, John the Baptist, was dead. Jesus wanted to find somewhere to be alone for a while, to grieve for John without being pestered by people. So he set off very early one morning to the far side of the Sea of Galilee.

To help him pray, he asked his twelve disciples to come with him. Together, they rowed across the sea, found a deserted hill, climbed it, and huddled close.

But they weren't alone for long. A fisherman had seen Jesus crossing the sea at dawn. He told a friend, who told his parents, and soon the news spread far and wide.

A great crowd followed and gradually gathered on the hillside around Jesus and his disciples. Jesus, knowing that they had come to hear him preach, stood up, and began to speak. He talked about John, and how he had gone to live with God. He explained as much as he could about the wonders of the Kingdom of Heaven.

Loaves and Fish

By the time he finished talking, the sun was starting to go down. The disciples hadn't eaten all day, and they were feeling tired and hungry. They realized that the people who had followed them must be starving, too.

Jesus quietly asked one of his disciples a question. "Philip, where do you think we can find enough food to feed all these people?"

Philip was surprised. He thought Jesus had an answer for everything. Perhaps it was a test. "I don't know, Jesus," he replied. "Even if we put all our money together, we'd only have enough to buy a loaf of bread for ourselves."

Another disciple, Andrew, chimed in. "There's a boy in the crowd who has five loaves of bread and two fish. It's a start – but it's hardly enough to feed the

whole crowd. Why, there must be at least five
thousand here!"

"Ask the boy to bring his food to me," said Jesus.
Andrew was confused, but he did as he was told.

Jesus took the bread and the fish and held them
up to God. He said a prayer of thanks, and then gave

one fish each to Philip and Andrew, sharing the loaves among the other disciples.

"Ask the people to sit together in groups of fifty," he said. "Then break off a piece of bread and a strip of fish for everyone."

The disciples started handing out the food. To their amazement, they found that every single person had plenty to eat. They were even more astonished at the end of the meal.

"Would you gather up the crumbs?" Jesus asked them – and they collected enough to fill a basket each.

The Good Samaritan

"What must I do to inherit eternal life?" a man asked Jesus one day. It seemed a simple enough question, but Jesus knew he had to be very careful with his answer. The man was an expert in Jewish law. One little mistake and Jesus risked angering the chief priests of Jerusalem and the Pharisees.

"What is written in the law?" Jesus replied cautiously. "How would *you* interpret it?"

The Good Samaritan

The lawyer puffed out his chest and rattled off the answer that was familiar to everyone listening. "Why, that you should love the Lord your God with all your heart and with all your soul and with all your strength and with all your mind, of course," he said. "And that you should love other people as yourself."

"Well then, you already have the answer," Jesus replied, smiling gently. "What you say is correct. If you do this, you will inherit eternal life."

The man frowned. He had no intention of letting Jesus off that lightly. "But tell me teacher, who are these 'other people' I should love?" he asked, looking around at the small group that had gathered, a self-satisfied smile on his face.

Jesus sighed, and then replied...

"A Jewish man was making a journey along the

road from Jerusalem to Jericho, when he was attacked by robbers. They took all his possessions, even his clothes, and beat him until he was unconscious. In fact, for all they knew, he was dead.

As luck would have it, or so you might think, a priest happened to walk by. He paused for a moment, and looked at the man lying on the ground. The man was clearly badly hurt, but what if this were a trick?

'What if some robbers have beaten him up and left him as bait?' the priest thought. 'If I stop, they might leap out and attack and rob me too!'

Besides, the man looked dead. If he touched a dead person, he, as a priest, would become unclean and be unable to carry out his religious duties. He *had* just been to Jerusalem and finished those duties

for the week, but even so...
The priest hurriedly
crossed over to the other
side of the road and
continued on his way
to Jericho.

A long, hot hour later,
the man was beginning to
come to. His eyes were so swollen he
couldn't open them, and his mouth felt as if it were
filled with sand. But he could hear someone
approaching.

This man was a Levite, a highly respected religious
man. The Levite didn't seem to hear the weak groan
that came from the man's mouth. Nor did he see the
man's feeble attempt to move his arm – but he didn't

look that hard. After one brief glance, he crossed over onto the other side of the road, just as the priest had done, and continued on his way.

Yet another agonizing hour later, the sun was going down and it was beginning to get very cold. And then a Samaritan came riding down the road on his donkey.

Now, everyone knows that the Samaritans and Jews loathe each other but, when he saw the man, this Samaritan jumped from his donkey and rushed over. He knelt down and felt for the man's pulse. He was still alive.

The Samaritan happened to be carrying bottles of olive oil and wine in his bag. He quickly opened them, cleaned the wounds with the wine, and gently rubbed oil onto them to help them heal. He ripped strips of cloth from the edge of his own cloak to bind the man's wounds. And then, carefully, he lifted the man onto his donkey and took him to an inn further down the road.

The Samaritan paid for a room and, even though he was in a hurry to continue his journey, he stayed there all night to look after the man. The next day, he gave the innkeeper two gold coins and asked that he look after the injured man until he was well enough to travel again. 'I'll look in on my way back,' he promised the innkeeper. 'If you spend more than those two coins, I will pay you the extra.'"

Jesus paused, looking at the attentive faces of his audience. "Now," he said. "Which of those three men do you think showed true love for others?" His glance fell on the lawyer.

"The man who showed mercy," the lawyer replied, looking rather shame-faced.

"Well, then," Jesus said. "Go and do the same yourself."

The Prodigal Son

"Shhh!" hissed a man who had come to listen to Jesus. "Stop muttering at the back!"

Jesus heard the disturbance and broke off from speaking to the crowd. "Is everything all right?" he asked.

"Well…" someone on the back row began nervously, "…we're Pharisees. We always obey God's laws to the very smallest detail."

"I'm glad to hear it," said Jesus. "So what's the problem?"

A more senior Pharisee butted in, "Surely *we* should be God's chosen ones, yet here you are talking to anyone and everyone who comes to listen to you – even greedy tax collectors and criminals."

"Yes, we spend all our time doing what God asks and where does all this obedience get us?" said the first Pharisee, feeling bolder. "You treat us just the same as those scoundrels!"

"Let me tell you a story about forgiveness..." said Jesus, and began...

"There was once a farmer who had two sons. He worked hard on his land and became rich. The elder son worked tirelessly with him on the farm, but the younger son was lazy and impatient. He decided he'd rather do something else.

'Father, when you die, half of what you have will be mine,' he said, one day. 'So why don't you just give it to me now?'

The Prodigal Son

His father was surprised and a little upset. 'What son asks for his inheritance early?' he wondered. 'Still, perhaps I should give him a chance to prove himself.' And he decided to grant the request.

'Great!' said the younger son, without even pausing to thank his father. 'I'd better say goodbye then. I'm done with life on this boring old farm – I'm off to the city.' With that, he packed up and left.

The city was the perfect place to enjoy spending money, especially if you hadn't really earned it.

First, the son bought a huge mansion, filling it with dozens of servants. Then he went shopping and bought the very best of everything. Every night, he threw extravagant parties for hundreds of people. 'This is the life,' he thought. 'I'm rich *and* popular!'

But keeping up such a luxurious lifestyle was

expensive, and it wasn't long before his father's money ran out.

'Oh well, time to get a job, I suppose,' he decided, begrudgingly. But when he asked for work around the city, he was met with the same response.

'Sorry... After the poor harvest this year I'm struggling to get by. I can't afford to take on any more staff.'

With no job to pay his bills, the younger son had to sell everything he'd bought. He couldn't even afford to feed himself, let alone host lavish feasts for other people. Dressed in rags, he wandered the streets begging for money or food, but the city was so poor that no one had anything to spare.

Finally, a poor farmer outside the city offered him work. 'I need someone to look after my pigs,' he said.

The Prodigal Son

'Pigs?' said the younger son, who had spent his life avoiding hard work. 'But they'll be smelly and dirty and... ugh, I can't bear to think about it.'

'So I'll find someone else then?' said the farmer.

'Oh... um... no, no, I'll take it,' said the son. He was so desperate that he had no choice.

Every day, he worked from sun up until sun down feeding the pigs their slop and cleaning up the sty. To make things worse, he was barely given enough food to survive himself.

'May I share the pigs' slop?' he asked the farmer.

'Absolutely not!' came the reply. 'We don't have a spoonful to spare.'

One evening, tired and

filthy after another long day, he remembered how life had been on his father's farm. 'Even the servants there were fed properly...' he recalled, wistfully. 'I know,' he thought, 'I'll go home.'

He set off the very next day. Along the way he thought long and hard about the mistakes he had made. 'Father was so kind, but I squandered everything he gave me. I'm not fit to be his son. All I can do now is hope that he might take me in as one of his servants.'

After a tiring journey, and with his head hung low in shame, he finally reached the farm. But as he approached, he had a shock. His father, who had seen him from a distance, burst out of the house and ran to greet him.

'You've come home! You've come home!' cried the

father, embracing his son.

'Father, I've wasted everything – I'm not worthy of being your son...' the young man started, but he was cut off before he could apologize further.

'Rejoice! My son is home,' his father shouted, pushing his son inside the house. 'Servants! Dress him in the finest robes and jewels. Tonight we'll have a great feast, with music and dancing all night long.'

The banquet that night was magnificent. Guests came from miles around, and the most tender and succulent meat from the farm was cooked and served.

But one person was far from happy.

'It's not fair,' the older brother complained.

'What's the matter, son?' asked his father.

'First my brother demanded money from you, then he wasted it like a fool in the city,' replied his son, crossly.

'Ah, well...' began the father, but his son hadn't finished.

'...and to make things worse, the minute he comes back you fling your arms around him and serve up the fatted calf – the best meat we have – at a banquet to celebrate his return. It's as if he hasn't done anything wrong!'

'Son, please...' said the father, trying to calm his son down.

The son continued, but his anger was turning to sadness, '...and meanwhile I've been toiling away on this farm for years on end. For nothing. You've never given me so much as a scrawny old goat to eat with my friends,' he finished.

His father looked at him solemnly. 'You are my oldest son,' he said. 'Everything I have is yours. Never forget that. I know your brother has made mistakes. He left us and was wasteful and reckless – a truly prodigal young man. But none of that matters now. The important thing is that he has returned. That is why I am so happy. We must welcome him with open arms and celebrate, because he was lost and now is found.'"

And with that, Jesus' story was finished. From then on, the Pharisees at the back kept quiet.

Jesus the Healer

"Whoever thinks they are the poorest, most worthless wretches around, God loves you the most!" Jesus called out to a large crowd that had gathered on the mountain slopes beside Galilee.

With words such as these, Jesus attracted thousands of followers. Soon, people who had never even met him started spreading stories that he could work miracles and heal the sick.

In fact, although Jesus had performed several miracles, he hadn't healed anyone. So he was taken by surprise when, one day, a stranger stumbled up to him, begging, "Heal me!"

"Stay back!" warned Peter. "Look at that man's bandages. He must have leprosy. If he comes too close we'll get sick ourselves." But Jesus was not afraid.

"What do you want?" he asked the man.

The man pulled down the sheaf of bandages that covered his face. His cheeks were scarred with red marks, and his skin was an unhealthy shade of green. Looking straight at Jesus, he said, "You're the one called Jesus, aren't you? Everyone is talking about you."

"What do they say?" asked Jesus.

"They say you're a healer. I'm dying from my leprosy, but if you touch me you can make me well."

Jesus placed both his hands on the man's head and said a prayer. Immediately, the man's skin began to glow with life, and the sores on his face vanished. He knelt down before Jesus, crying, "Thank you, thank you!" over and over again.

Jesus helped him up. "It is your own belief that has made you well," he said. "Please, go and say a prayer of thanks to God – but don't tell anyone that I did this."

The man agreed to keep quiet, and ran off.

"That was amazing, Jesus!" said Peter. "I didn't know you could heal people."

Jesus said nothing.

"It's getting dark," Peter went on. "Won't you come back to my house tonight?" But when they arrived, they found the house locked up. Concerned, Peter knocked sharply on the door. After some minutes, his wife opened the door a crack. Peter and Jesus could see she had been crying.

"Oh Peter," she said, flinging the door wide open, "it's Mother. She's come down with such a raging fever, I'm afraid she won't last the night!"

While Peter comforted his wife, Jesus walked past them and into the bedroom. He sat at the edge of the bed where the old woman lay shivering, and laid a hand on her forehead. Immediately, the fever broke.

Soon, she was able to sit up and talk. "I feel so much better," she said with a smile, "I think I'll prepare supper." Peter and his wife cried out with joy.

Jesus was happy, too – but he knew that from then on, his life would never be the same.

Sure enough, by the next evening the story of how he had cured a fever spread. Before long, Jesus found that wherever he went, people were asking him to treat their ailments, big and small.

Jesus the Healer

Whenever he could, Jesus helped. He opened the ears of a deaf man. He made a kind of mud that restored sight to the blind. And he drove demons out of people's minds to heal their madness.

Once, he was in a friend's house, telling a story. The house was packed with people listening intently, including several priests who were eager to find out for themselves what kind of a preacher Jesus was. A crowd had even gathered on the street outside the window, so that they could hear him too.

Right in the middle of his story, Jesus stopped talking. A strange banging was coming from the ceiling. Everyone looked up and watched as a trickle of dust fell to the floor. All of a sudden, a section of the roof was entirely lifted off, revealing a group of people standing in the sunlight.

Jesus the Healer

As Jesus was squinting up at the sky, two men lowered a stretcher into the room. On top lay a man who was paralyzed. For some years, he had been unable to move his arms or legs.

Jesus was impressed by their efforts to get the man to see him, despite the crowds. He looked down at the man on the stretcher and said, "Stand, pick up your stretcher, and walk."

Without a word, the man stood, picked up his stretcher and walked from the room. The crowd gasped. The priests rose to their feet, astonished. It was the first time they had seen Jesus perform a miracle. Some of them were excited to witness such a display of power, but others were afraid, believing that Jesus was a threat to their authority.

Jesus became so famous that the wealthiest people

in Judea came looking for him. One of them, a man named Jairus, sent a servant to ask Jesus to heal his daughter, who was desperately ill.

Jesus had to push his way through a great throng of people to reach Jairus' house. Halfway across the road, Jesus stopped.

"Someone touched me!" he exclaimed.

"What do you mean, Jesus?" asked Andrew. "People are pressing into us from all sides, of course somebody touched you."

"I felt something more than that," Jesus explained. "It was as if some of my power left my body."

"F-forgive me," stuttered a voice. Jesus and Andrew looked down to see a woman kneeling on the ground, sobbing.

"It was me," she wept. "I touched you. I'm just an

old widow, alone and sickly. You're so important and busy, I didn't think you would stop to help me, but I thought to myself, 'If only I can touch his cloak, I will be well again.'"

Jesus smiled at the woman and then turned and spoke to the crowd. "This woman believed I could heal her if she only touched my cloak." He looked at her again and gently said, "Get up and go home. Let your faith be an inspiration to everyone."

The woman left, smiling and uttering prayers of thanks, and Jesus hurried on to Jairus' house. He found the house silent as a grave.

Jairus was waiting outside, but before he could speak, a servant pulled him back and said, "Master, don't trouble this great healer any more. It's too late."

Jesus heard the servant and said to Jairus, "He is

acting as if your daughter has died, but I promise you, she is only asleep."

The servant sneered at Jesus. "How dare you get my master's hopes up! Do you take me for a fool?"

Jesus ignored the servant and went into the house, where he found the girl upstairs, lying in her bed. From outside, everyone heard Jesus' voice through the bedroom window, saying, "Wake up, little one."

And the girl got up, going downstairs to see her parents. "I told you she was only sleeping," Jesus said. "She's hungry, too. I'd give her something to eat."

Jairus' servants began to spread the tale that Jesus hadn't simply cured the child's illness – he had actually brought a dead girl back to life. The chief priests didn't really believe this, but they didn't like the idea at all.

Jesus the Healer

There was one day in each week when people did not pester Jesus to heal their wounds and cure their diseases – Saturday. The Jews kept Saturday, the Sabbath day, as a day of rest. The rule was that no one should do any form of work, whether it was carrying water from a well, buying or selling things in the market, or even performing a miracle.

On one particular Saturday, a huddle of Pharisees decided to try to trick Jesus. They found a man who needed healing, and brought him to a temple in Jerusalem where they knew Jesus was preaching. The man had been born with a withered hand and the Pharisees made certain that Jesus could see it.

Jesus watched them shuffle into the temple. He could tell they weren't really interested in helping the man get better. "Stand up," Jesus said to the man with the withered hand. "Show everyone your hand."

The man held his bad arm as high as he could. Everyone could see his hand hanging there, limp and useless. But would Jesus dare to heal him – and break the rule of the Sabbath?

"We keep Saturday as the Sabbath day to show our respect to God," Jesus declared. "Now, I ask you all this question: doesn't it show respect to God to do a good deed? Even on the Sabbath day, would it really be better to let a man die or go on suffering if you could help him in some way?"

No one replied, because the answer was so obvious. Of course it was better to do good.

Jesus spoke again, this time directly to the man with the withered hand. "Stretch out your hand," he said, and the man did. It was completely cured.

"You may go," Jesus said to him.

The Pharisees seethed with rage, furious they had
been outwitted, and began plotting ways to silence
Jesus – for good.

Jesus decided it would be safest to leave Jerusalem
and stay somewhere quiet. But only a few weeks later,
he was caught in a dilemma. He didn't want to go
anywhere near Jerusalem and the chief priests for a

while, but he had just heard that one of his closest friends, Lazarus, was dying. And Lazarus lived in Bethany, barely a mile outside Jerusalem.

Jesus and his disciples argued about what to do for two whole days. Finally, Jesus announced, "It is time. I must go and wake Lazarus up."

"Lazarus is asleep?"

"No," said Jesus solemnly. "Lazarus is dead."

By now, the disciples had seen Jesus perform many wonders, even cure Jairus' seriously ill daughter – though he had insisted she had merely been sleeping. Could Jesus really raise someone from the dead?

"We have to go with him," said Thomas, one of the disciples. "We might not be able to help Lazarus, but we can't leave Jesus on his own. He could be arrested, even killed!"

Jesus and his disciples made their way to Bethany that night. Lazarus' sisters, Martha and Mary, crept out of town to meet them.

"I wish you had come sooner," Martha said to Jesus. "I know you could have saved Lazarus' life."

"Martha, Lazarus will rise again," Jesus promised.

"I know, Jesus. He will rise again at the end of the world, when everyone comes out of their graves to be with God."

"No, that's not what I meant," Jesus replied. "I have the power to give life – even to people who have died. Do you believe me, Martha? Mary, you know who I really am, don't you?"

"Yes, Jesus. You are God's son, come to save all people. I believe in you," Mary replied, as the sisters led Jesus to the cave where their brother's body lay.

The disciples were waiting nearby. They merged with crowds of mourners from Bethany, who had gathered by the tomb. Everyone watched as Jesus broke down and wept.

"Take away the stone," Jesus said at last.

"But Jesus," Martha said, "Lazarus has been dead for three days now."

"Martha, do you still not believe in me?"

Martha said nothing. She and Mary rolled away the stone blocking the tomb, and Jesus peered into the gloomy cave.

"Lazarus, come out!" he shouted.

Some minutes later, the sound of shuffling footsteps echoed through the cave. Lazarus was coming. Before they could see him properly, the crowds recoiled at the dreadful stench. And then, he

appeared – a phantom of death. He was wrapped in the white sheets used to prepare a body for burial, but he was walking. Lazarus was alive!

"Take off his bandages, and let him go," Jesus said to the disciples. The disciples and half of the crowd reacted with cheers of joy. But the rest were afraid. Some of them ran away to tell the chief priests what had happened and Jesus knew that his days were numbered.

The Easter Story

The Easter Story

Jesus and his disciples were journeying to Jerusalem for the festival of Passover, which commemorated the Jews' freedom from slavery in Egypt, centuries before.

On the way, they stopped near the village of Bethany. "Go into the village," Jesus told two of his disciples. "There you will find a donkey that has never been ridden. Bring it to me."

The disciples soon found the donkey and led it to Jesus. They laid their cloaks on the donkey's back to make a soft seat and Jesus rode into Jerusalem, his disciples close behind.

Cheering crowds lined the streets. Everyone was overjoyed to see Jesus. Some people spread their cloaks on the ground for his donkey to walk on. Others cut leaves from nearby palm trees and laid them alongside the cloaks.

At the Temple, Jesus and his disciples stopped to pray, before returning to Bethany for the night.

When they came back the next morning, they were appalled by what they saw. The courtyard in front of the Temple was full of traders selling cows, doves and sheep, while others were changing money.

Shaking with rage, Jesus marched up to the money-changers and threw their stalls over. Still angry, he tipped over the traders' stalls too.

"God's house is a house of prayer!" he bellowed, driving them away, "but you have turned it into a den of thieves."

When the traders were gone, Jesus turned to the crowds who had gathered, telling them about God and healing those who were sick.

It wasn't long before news of the outburst reached the chief priests of the Temple. "The people should be listening to us, not this Jesus," they fumed, and decided to arrest him. But Jesus was a popular preacher. They would have to wait until he was alone, in case the people tried to protect him.

One of Jesus' disciples, Judas Iscariot, discovered what the chief priests were planning.

"If I tell you when Jesus is alone, what will you give me?" Judas asked.

The priests offered him thirty pieces of silver.

"I'll do it," Judas promised.

A few days later, Jesus and his disciples were celebrating the Feast of Passover. Before they sat down to eat, Jesus washed his disciples' feet. "Remember, a master is no more important than his servant," he told them.

As the meal began, Jesus made a shocking announcement. "One of you, my trusted disciples, will shortly betray me."

His disciples were horrified. "Never!" they cried.

"It will be the one I give this bread to," said Jesus, tearing a piece from a loaf, and handing it to Judas.

Judas fled from the table and ran into the night.

As the rest of the disciples sat in stunned silence, Jesus handed a piece of bread to each of them.

"Eat this bread which is my body, and remember me," he said. Then he passed them a cup of wine. "This is my blood which I give for you and many people," he said. "Drink it and remember me."

Later that night, Jesus and his disciples walked to Gethsemane, a garden of olive trees. On the way, Jesus told his friends they would soon desert him.

Peter frowned in disbelief. "Not me," he insisted.

"You will swear you don't know me three times before the sun rises tomorrow morning," Jesus replied.

At the garden, Jesus left his disciples watching for guards, while he found a quiet place to pray. When he returned, they were asleep.

"Couldn't you stay awake for just one hour?" he asked sadly. Twice more he left them, and twice more he returned to find them asleep. As he woke them up for the third time, Judas appeared with the chief priests and some Temple guards.

Judas walked up to Jesus and kissed him on the

cheek. "This is the man you want," he said.

The disciples were so frightened they ran away, just as Jesus had foretold.

The guards marched Jesus to the palace of Caiaphas, the High Priest, to stand trial.

Outside the palace, Peter joined the gathering crowd. Three different people recognized him as one of Jesus' friends. But each time they spoke, Peter swore he didn't know Jesus.

The sky filled with the rosy glow of dawn, and Peter recalled Jesus' words. Feeling bitterly ashamed, he ran away and hid, tears streaming

down his face.

Inside the palace, Jesus' trial began, with the chief priests and Jewish leaders listening intently. Various witnesses had been bribed to tell lies about Jesus, but their stories didn't match up. No one could prove that he had done anything wrong.

At last, Caiaphas asked Jesus if he was the Son of God.

"I am," Jesus said in a quiet voice.

"He claims to be equal with God, and that is blasphemy," Caiaphas declared.

"Ha! Blasphemer!" spat those watching.

"I sentence him to death," announced the High Priest, though he knew he needed the permission of Pontius Pilate, the Roman Governor, before he could execute anyone.

The chief priests also knew perfectly well that Pilate would never kill a man for blasphemy against their God, so they accused him of treason.

Pilate soon realized that Jesus was innocent, but he didn't want to upset the Jewish leaders by setting him free. He thought he saw a way out. During Passover, it was the custom to free one prisoner, and Pilate offered to free Jesus.

"I can free Jesus or I can free the convicted murderer, Barabbas," Pilate called to the crowd waiting outside his palace. But the chief priests persuaded the crowd to turn against Jesus.

"Free Barabbas! Crucify Jesus!" came the shouts.

Pilate despaired. He called for a bowl of water and washed his hands, saying, "I wash my hands of guilt in this man's death. This is your doing."

Roman soldiers led Jesus away and dressed him in a purple robe and a crown made from thorns.

"Hail, King of the Jews," they jeered, beating him. Then they dressed him in his own clothes, and

dragged him away to be crucified.

Jesus was made to carry a huge wooden cross through the streets of Jerusalem. Exhausted, and weak from the beatings he had received, Jesus struggled. Again and again, he stumbled and fell under the weight of the cross.

Eventually, one of the soldiers called to a foreigner named Simon who was watching the procession. "You! Carry the cross for him," he ordered.

The Easter Story

Simon and Jesus staggered on, until they reached a place outside the city named Golgotha. Here, soldiers nailed Jesus to the cross by his hands and feet.

Jesus looked down at the soldiers and people who had gathered below. They began to taunt him.

"If you really are the Son of God," they shouted, "why don't you save yourself?"

"Forgive them, Father," he prayed. "They don't know what they're saying."

His gaze fell on his mother, Mary, standing near the cross with John, one of his disciples. "Take care of her for me," he asked John.

At midday, the sky grew dark for three hours. "My God, why have You abandoned me?" cried Jesus. Then he bowed his head. "Father, I put my spirit into Your hands," he whispered, and died.

The Easter Story

At that moment the ground shook. Everyone was frightened.

"This man really was the Son of God," cried a Roman soldier.

The soldiers took Jesus down from the cross and a rich man, Joseph from Arimathea, who believed in Jesus, wrapped his body in a linen cloth.

Along with some of Jesus' friends, Joseph carried the body to a garden outside Jerusalem. They placed it in a tomb cut into a rock and rolled a large, heavy stone in front of the entrance.

By now it was sunset on Friday evening and the Jewish Sabbath had begun. Joseph and the others left the garden, planning to bury Jesus properly after the Sabbath had ended on Saturday evening.

On Sunday morning, Mary Magdalene, one of

Jesus' friends, returned to the tomb with two of his other friends to finish the burial preparations. They were shocked to see the stone had been rolled away.

Suddenly, a figure in white appeared. "Jesus is not here," said the man. "He is alive."

Sure enough, Jesus' body was gone.

The three women ran to tell the disciples, and Peter and John rushed to the tomb to see for themselves.

After they left, Mary Magdalene returned. As she knelt weeping by the empty tomb, she heard a familiar voice at her side.

"Mary," said the voice.

Mary looked up to see Jesus standing over her.

"Go and tell my friends you've seen me," said Jesus, "and that soon I'll be with my Father in Heaven."

Over the forty days that followed, Jesus often returned to his friends.

The final time he appeared to the disciples was when they were walking on the Mount of Olives outside Jerusalem.

"Tell the whole world the good news," Jesus said to them. "All those who trust in me, and truly regret their wrongs, will be forgiven. I will give each of them a new life, and I shall always be with you." Then the disciples watched in awe as a cloud surrounded Jesus and gently carried him up to Heaven.

Map of the New Testament Lands

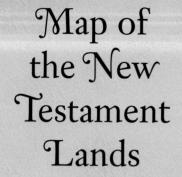

Mediterranean
Sea

Samaria
(Land of the
Samaritans)

Arimathea
·

Judea

Galilee

Cana

Capernaum ·
· Bethsaida

Sea of
Galilee

Nazareth

About 5 days' journey

River Jordan

Jericho ·

Jerusalem · · Bethany
Bethlehem ·

Dead Sea

Egypt

Who's Who in the New Testament

Caiaphas: High Priest of the Jews, and an enemy of Jesus, he led the plotting against him

Elizabeth: cousin of Mary, and mother of John the Baptist, though she thought she was too old for children

 Gabriel: an angel, and God's chief messenger to people on Earth

Herod: king of the Jews when Jesus was born

Jesus: the Son of God, but also a Jew with human parents, Mary and Joseph

Jews: descendants of the Israelites, who lived in the Roman province known as Judea

 John the Baptist: Jesus' cousin, who baptized people by washing them in the River Jordan

 Joseph: a carpenter from Nazareth, and the human father of Jesus

Lazarus: one of Jesus' best friends, who died and was brought back to life by Jesus

 Mary: human mother of Jesus, who stayed with him throughout his life

Mary Magdalene: a close friend of Jesus and the twelve disciples

Pharisees: junior priests who worked for Caiaphas, and were enemies of Jesus

Pontius Pilate: a Roman official in charge of Judea, he sentenced Jesus to death

Samaritans: a sect of Jews who lived in Samaria and were enemies of the Jews of Judea and Galilee

The Twelve Disciples

The four Gospels talk about twelve men who were close to Jesus and were known as his disciples. Some of them have nicknames, and others are known by completely different names in different Gospels.

Simon, nicknamed 'Peter'

Andrew, Simon (Peter)'s brother

James and **John**, nicknamed 'the sons of Zebedee'

Philip

Thomas

Judas Iscariot

Simon, nicknamed 'the zealot'

James, nicknamed 'son of Alphaeus'

Nathaniel, also called Bartholomew

Thaddeus, also called Jude

Matthew, also called Levi

Matthias, who became a disciple after Judas died

Acknowledgements

Stories retold by: Sam Baer, Rachel Firth, Alex Frith, Rosie Hore, Jonathan Melmoth, Russell Punter, Louie Stowell and Abigail Wheatley

Bible expert: The Revd. Dr. Nicholas Cranfield FSA
Edited by Lesley Sims

Designed by Laura Nelson
Digital imaging by Nick Wakeford and John Russell

First published in 2015 by Usborne Publishing Ltd., 83-85 Saffron Hill, London EC1N 8RT, England. www.usborne.com. Copyright © 2015 Usborne Publishing Limited. The name Usborne and the devices ♀⊕ are Trade Marks of Usborne Publishing Ltd. All rights reserved.
No part of this publication may be reproduced, stored in a retrieval system, or transmitted in any form or by any means, electronic, mechanical, photocopying, recording or otherwise, without the prior permission of the publisher. First published in America in 2015. UE.